This book belongs to:

. . . .

Praise for

'A monstrously funny new voice'
Maz Evans, author of *Who Let the Gods Out?*

'Monster Hunting For Beginners is the best kind of
children's book: funny, fast paced and bursting with
adventure. The brilliant pictures match the story
perfectly. You'll gobble this book up!'
Jenny McLachlan, author of *The Land of Roar*

'Ian Mark has created a magnificently hilarious
masterpiece of monster proportions. I howled with
laughter! The next in the series better come out soon,
or I'll hunt him down like I might the
Crusted Hairy Snot Nibbler'
**Jenny Pearson, author of *The Super Miraculous
Journey of Freddie Yates***

'A funny, fast-paced tale for young adventurers,
with gags sharper than a dragon's front teeth'
David Solomons, author of *My Brother is a Superhero*

'A rib-tickling comic adventure let down by an all too
familiar negative depiction of man-eating monsters'
Cosmopolitroll*

'This so-called comedy for young humans only
underlines the oppression that evil monsters have
to face on a daily basis'
The Three-Headed Guardian**

'Crackin'!'
Kraken Monthly***

* Actually David Solomons
** David Solomons again
*** This one is an ACTUAL MONSTER.
Only joking! It's David Solomons.

MONSTER HUNTING
for BEGINNERS

First published in Great Britain 2021 by Farshore
An imprint of HarperCollins*Publishers*
1 London Bridge Street, London SE1 9GF

www.farshore.co.uk

HarperCollins*Publishers*
1st Floor, Watermarque Building, Ringsend Road
Dublin 4, Ireland

ISBN 978 0 7555 0194 6

Printed and bound in the UK using 100% renewable electricity
at CPI Group (UK) Ltd

1

A CIP catalogue record for this title is available from the British Library.

MIX
Paper from
responsible sources
FSC® C007454

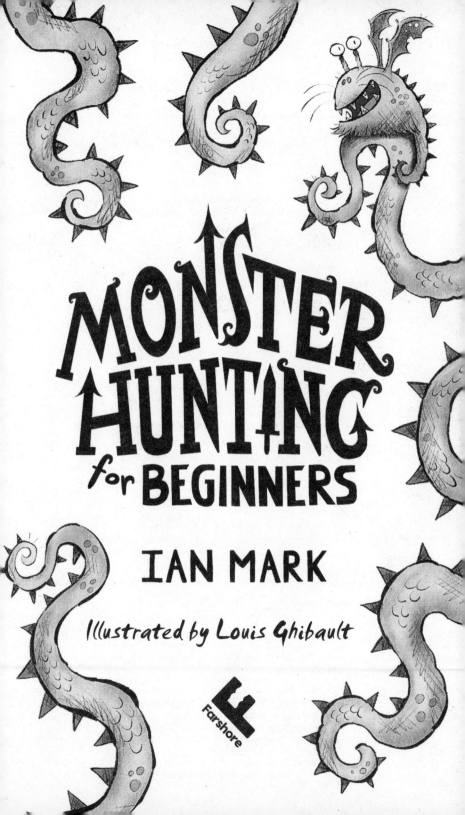

MONSTER HUNTING
for BEGINNERS

IAN MARK

Illustrated by Louis Ghibault

Farshore

First Things First

Monster hunting isn't as easy as it looks.

I should know.

My name's Jack, and I'm a monster hunter.

I know what you're thinking. That kid can't be a monster hunter. Look at him. He couldn't fight a cold, never mind the sort of bloodthirsty creatures you'd expect to find in the pages of a book rather than in real life.

I get that a LOT.

I'm small for my age.

I wear glasses.

I'm clumsy.

I'm not built for trouble.

My hair is too long and is

always falling over my eyes at the wrong moment.

But it's true. I can prove it. Here is me doing battle with a Kraken. (The Kraken is the one on the left.)

This is me trying to hypnotise a three-headed bogeyman with an eyeball tied to a string of mouldy spaghetti. (Trust me, you don't want to know all the horrible details. I still have nightmares about it sometimes.)

And here I am having a wrestling match with . . . well, I'm not sure what that is. Some sort of shapeless blob with too many mouths.*

Not all monsters have names. That's one thing I've learned since taking up the job.

I've also discovered that you should never say "good doggie" to a Hellhound when it's in a bad mood.

That's why I'm running very fast in this picture.

In fact, I was running so fast, I'd already run away before the picture could be taken.

(Sorry about that.)

* In case you're wondering, I lost. It's not easy holding on to a blob long enough to make it admit defeat.

But I'm getting ahead of myself. Begin at the beginning, isn't that what everyone says? I've already broken that rule, but it's still not bad advice. Let's start again.

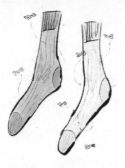

In The Beginning

I wasn't always a monster hunter.

To begin with, I was just a baby.* You can't fight monsters in a dirty nappy.

It's too messy.

Soon after that, I was sent to school. There I had to sit still for hours every day, learning my ABCs, together with all the other letters of the alphabet, because apparently you can't get far in life only knowing the first three.

I was even forced to do a thing called **Long Division**, which I've since found out is banned as a form of torture in at least seven countries.

* Most people are. To begin with.

It didn't leave much free time for playing hide and seek with Hobgoblins.

Back then, I'd never actually seen a monster with my own eyes – or anyone else's eyes, for that matter. But I had good reasons to believe that they were real. The other children laughed at me when I tried to tell them that the world was as full of monsters as a cheese sandwich is full of cheese. I didn't care.

I was happy to sit by myself during break, doodling strange animals in the margins of my school book. Somehow I always knew that I was destined for **Bigger Things**. There had to be more to life than going to school and doing my homework and cleaning my room!

Let's just say I had a **Taste For Adventure.*** The only problem was that nothing exciting ever happened to me.

There were two reasons for that.

The first reason was called Dad.

He wasn't bad, as Dads go. He didn't make

---

* *I also had a taste for sausage rolls, but this isn't the time to get distracted by thoughts of food.*

me stand on my head for three hours for my pocket money, or take me to the dentist as a treat on my birthday.

He just wasn't very adventurous, that's all.

The most daring thing Dad ever did was wear odd socks on Thursdays. He wouldn't even let me keep a pet snail, because he said they were too ferocious and might bite me. Dad worried about **EVERYTHING**.

That was because of the second reason.

She was called Mum.

It was Mum who'd first told to me **The Truth About Monsters**. When I was small*, she was constantly telling me stories about the strange, wonderful, terrifying creatures that wandered the hidden places of the earth.

Especially dragons. I longed to see a dragon more than anything.

Well, almost anything.

What I MOST wanted to see was Mum

* *Smaller to be more precise.*

again, but I couldn't, because she'd died.

Here's my favourite photograph of us all on holiday when I was a baby. (It was taken on a Thursday, as you can tell by Dad's socks.) It made me sad to look at sometimes, but happy too, because it helped me to remember when she'd been here, even if she wasn't now.

After she died, Dad had given up his job* to look after me, and he was what experts in the field – or children, as they're better known – call a **Bit Of A Party Pooper**. That means he

* *Whatever that was.*

8

was afraid of me doing anything in case I hurt myself . . . or worse. I get it! He'd lost Mum, and he didn't want to lose me too.

But it was frustrating. Sometimes I just wanted to **Go Wild** for a while, and you can't do that with a Dad fussing at your shoulder every minute saying, "Don't run too fast, Jack, you'll trip over your shoelaces" or "You mustn't sit there, Jack, you'll get piles."*

What I didn't know is that my boring life doing boring things every boring minute of every boring day of the boring year was about to get very not boring indeed.

* Piles are really nasty things you get on your bum. Grown-ups are convinced that sitting down anywhere damp and chilly for five seconds will make them sprout up faster than cress on a wet paper towel.

Knock, Knock

The day that everything changed began like any other. As usual, I was woken up by the sound of my shiny brass alarm clock going off. As usual, I groaned and clamped the pillow over my head in the hope of getting five minutes' more sleep.

Dad called me precisely thirty-three seconds later, as he usually did, to tell me that breakfast was ready, and I trudged downstairs drowsily in the usual way to eat it.

I set off for school shortly afterwards, only to be called back by Dad, who pointed out that I was still wearing my pyjamas.*

* That, I'm glad to say, wasn't usual at all.

I quickly flung on the right clothes, then dashed the rest of the way to school, hoping that I wouldn't get into trouble for being late.

(I did.)

In the hours that followed, I was shouted at three times for staring out of the window, daydreaming about dragons, when I was meant to be learning why some places have volcanoes and some don't.*

I got into more trouble when Stanley Jenkins, who'd recently been elected Head Bully, dropped a worm down the back of my neck in the middle of a spelling test, making me jump to my feet with a scream.

The teacher demanded to know what was going on. Stanley Jenkins said that I'd begged him to do it to help cure my hiccups.

The teacher, being every bit as stupid as Stanley Jenkins, believed him.

The moment the bell rang to set me free, I grabbed my bag and ran home happily. It was

* I still don't know the reason. Like I said, I wasn't paying attention.

the end of another week. I couldn't wait to sit down with Dad in front of the TV with our regular Friday night supper of fish and chips.

Problem No. 1: When I got home, there were no chips waiting on the table.

Problem No. 2: There was no fish either.

Problem No. 3: There was also no Dad.

Which, when I thought about it, probably explained the first two problems.

I called his name.

No answer.

I checked every room.

The house was emptier than Stanley Jenkins' brain.

That wasn't like Dad.

Not.

At.

All.

He was ALWAYS waiting for me when I got home, and he ALWAYS asked me the same question: "How was school today?"*

---

* Why do parents do that? It's school. It's not like anything exciting ever happens there.

Trying not to worry, I kicked off my shoes, and settled down on the sofa to flick channels while I waited for him to return. I must have nodded off, because the next thing I remember it was nearly dark and there was a loud knocking at the door.

'Dad!' I said, jumping up and rubbing my eyes in confusion. "Where have you been?"

I opened the door to see THIS standing outside on the doorstep.

Who's there?

Scary, or what?

She said her name was Aunt Prudence.

Worse still, she said she was MY Aunt Prudence, and that she was moving in at once to look after me, whether I liked it or not.*

"I don't think I have an Aunt Prudence," I tried explaining politely, because I'd always been taught to **speak nicely to my elders** – even if they were glaring at me through their flying goggles as if I was something unpleasant that had been trodden into the carpet and wouldn't come out no matter how hard you scrubbed it. "Dad would have mentioned it. Are you sure you've come to the right house?"

* *Just to be clear, I didn't.*

"Of course I am, you confounded pest," she said. "Your idiot of a father's decided to go off on a round-the-world voyage and he's asked me to look after you until he gets back."

"But . . ." I started to say, because that absolutely did not sound like the sort of thing Dad would do, and I knew him better than she did. I knew him better than anyone.

"No buts!" she shouted, because no one listens to you when you're small and wear glasses. "All that butting will turn you into a goat! Now shut up and get out of my way. Boys' voices make my ears bleed."

Then she shoved me out of the way and barged right in without even wiping her feet, treading on my toes in her fearsome black hobnail boots as she passed.*

She immediately made herself at home by demanding that I put all my stuff out of sight to make more room for her (really quite enormous) collection of hobnail boots.

*I'm sure she did it on purpose when she saw that I was only wearing socks.

Soon it felt more like her home than mine, and that didn't feel like a home at all.

Aunt Prudence was very strict. She insisted that I eat all my meals with a knife and fork, even if it was soup, or cheese and onion crisps. She refused to let me watch cartoons on TV, only long documentaries about History – and if she'd known that those were my favourite programmes, then she wouldn't have let me watch them either.

I never saw her smile, and she once had to lie down in a dark room for an hour when she heard me laughing because it upset her so much. Jokes brought her out in a rash.

She had a note from the doctor to prove it.

There was no way Dad would have gone away and left me at the mercy of such a dreadful person if he could help it, even if she was my aunt.* She said she had proof it was true, but she never produced it, no matter how many times I asked.

* And I had Serious Doubts about that as well.

16

Instead, Aunt Prudence spent her days snooping round the house . . .

Opening cupboard doors . . .

Looking under beds . . .

Digging in the garden.

She was obviously looking for something, and I was determined to find out what it was.

A week after Dad's disappearance, I finally got a chance to do just that.

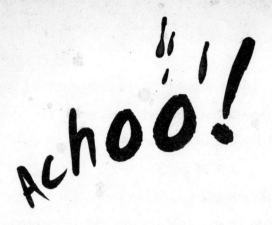

Achoo!

It was late at night, and I was lying in bed, trying hard to sleep. That isn't easy when your mind is churning round and round like a washing machine with too many dirty clothes inside. It's even harder when there's a strange noise above your head.

What was going on up there?

I got up and tiptoed on to the landing, then climbed the ladder to the attic

Up here was where Dad had stashed away Mum's things after she died. I hadn't been allowed in since. He told me that I should try to forget what she'd said about monsters being real and try to live an ordinary life instead. I hadn't been happy about it, but what could I do? Dad had the only key, and I was no good at picking locks with a bent paper clip.*

Aunt Prudence must have found the key during one of her searches of the house, because the hatch was now unlocked.

Peeking through the gap, I watched Aunt Prudence crawling on her hands and knees between huge teetering piles of boxes, as armies of spiders scuttled away in **Sheer Terror** at the sight of her. Each time she came to a new box, she tore it open and rummaged inside, flinging everything aside in Furious Indignation when she couldn't find what she was looking for, muttering under her breath all the while: "Where is it? Where is it?"

Dust was swirling about in the musty air as if it was trying to turn itself into a genie.

I made an effort not to sneeze.

It didn't help.

If there's one thing that's guaranteed to make you sneeze, it's trying not to. My nose twitched

---

* *I'd tried to do it many times.*

as if I was a rabbit, which I'm definitely not as you can tell from the pictures.

I rubbed it once.

I rubbed it twice.

Both times, I simply breathed in more dust.

The third time, my nose decided it had had enough. It exploded.*

The sneeze was mighty enough to bring Aunt Prudence to her feet. She promptly banged her head on the rafters.

"You!" she yelled.

She reached into the nearest box and grabbed the first thing that came to hand. That happened to be some sort of long silver horn. I didn't have time to wonder why there was a silver horn, long or otherwise, in our attic, before she hurled it straight at me.

I managed to shut the hatch at the last moment, or the blow would have sent my glasses flying, and my head with it.

Then I slid down the ladder as fast as I could,

* Though thankfully not the way a bomb would, or I'd have blown the roof off.

and sped to my room with Aunt Prudence in **Hot Pursuit**. Heart pounding, I locked myself inside, as she rattled the handle and snarled through the keyhole: "I'll get you in the morning, Jack. You see if I don't."

That's probably why I had what can only be described as **Mixed Feelings** when my alarm clock didn't go off the next day and I crept down the stairs late to find an Ogre sitting in the back garden getting ready to eat her.

Thwack!

I'd never
encountered a real
life monster in the
flesh before, unless
you include Aunt
Prudence, and I can't
think of a good reason why
you wouldn't.

So, when I tell you that he was the biggest
and scariest brute I'd ever seen in my life, that
probably isn't saying much.

But he was.

His skin was green and lumpy like nine-day-
old mould. He had disgusting yellow tusks that
looked as if they'd never heard of toothpaste,
let alone touched it in the last hundred years,

and he was wearing what had to be one of the world's top five most torn and dirtiest pairs of trousers.

Aunt Prudence was getting an even closer look at the Ogre than I was, because he'd picked her up tightly in his fist like a chocolate bar and was opening his mouth as if to bite off her head as she struggled to get free, kicking her legs in midair and crying: "Let me go!"

"Don't just stand there! Do something!" she shouted when she saw me.

If I'm honest, and I usually am, I couldn't help thinking that getting eaten would serve her right for being so mean. In fact, I felt a bit sorry for the Ogre, because someone as sour and nasty as Aunt Prudence was bound to give him a worse case of indigestion than a whole vinegar and raw onion pie right before bedtime.

Luckily for her, I'm not the sort

of boy who stands idly by while monsters eat people, not even foul-tempered aunts.

I ran inside and grabbed my school bag from the coat stand. Then I knelt down to see if there was anything in there that might help fight a ravenous, over-sized monster.

Conkers – not strong enough.

Pencils – not bad, but the tips were all broken, and I'd lost my sharpener.

A fur ball coughed up by a cat – EURGGGH, what was that doing there*?

Wait, what was this right at the bottom?

A catapult – just the thing!

The catapult had been a present from Dad for my last birthday.**

I'd been surprised when he gave it to me, because he normally didn't like me playing with anything more perilous than a rubber duck. Giving it to me wasn't his idea, he'd admitted. The catapult had once belonged to Mum. It was she who'd wanted me to have it.

* Fur balls are clumps of hair that form in cats' stomachs when they lick themselves clean. Cats love to vomit them out on to the cleanest bits of carpet.

** My tenth, since you ask, but it should really be the eleventh, because if the day that you're born isn't your first birthday, then what is? For some reason, though, they never count that one.

"You never know when it might come in handy, I suppose," were his precise words.

Today was that day.

Running back into the garden, I found a nice sharp rock, fitted it into the catapult and fired it hard at the Ogre's head.

The rock hit him right between the eyes.

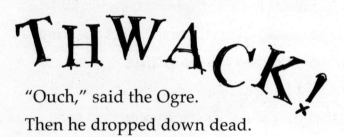

THWACK!

"Ouch," said the Ogre.

Then he dropped down dead.

All Fall Down

For a moment, I stood there, staring dumbly, unable to move, overwhelmed with a feeling that I can only describe as **panic**.*

I felt that I should say something, but "Oops" didn't seem the right word in the circumstances and "Sorry" was a bit late.

The only word I could think of was one of those words that children are not meant to say out loud, even when they have killed an Ogre.

What had I done?

I'd only meant to distract him long enough so that Aunt Prudence could escape from his clutches. Instead I'd . . . I'd . . . I'd killed him.

I felt sick.

Probably because that's what it was.

26

I felt scared.

I'd never killed an Ogre before.

I'd never killed an anything!

What made matters worse is that this Ogre had dropped down dead backwards, which meant that he landed on top of the house.

There was a huge CRASH . . . no, it was much bigger than that, more like a

and the air was filled with flying rubble and glass and bricks.

When the dust cleared, I saw that my house was completely destroyed.

"You blithering nincompoop!" cried Aunt Prudence, clambering to her feet and wiping the dirt from her flying goggles so that she could scowl at me more spitefully through them. "Look what you've done!"

She didn't even say thank you for saving her from having to spend the rest of the morning in an Ogre's belly. She simply turned on her heels

and stamped off down the road, yelling for
a taxi. I was left wondering how I was supposed
to clean up this mess when I couldn't even get
a dustpan and brush from under the stairs,
because the stairs weren't there any more, and
neither was anything else, except for a large
pile of rubble.

"That's what you get for trying to help
people," said a voice behind me. "If you ask me,
you should just let them all be eaten."

Little Black Book

I spun round to see who'd spoken.

There was nobody there.

"Down here," the voice said.

I looked down as instructed. There stood a little man with a shaggy beard and a red nose.

I'm small for my age, but he was small for any age. The top of his head only just reached past my knees, and he wore a battered tin helmet and a leather tunic with a large collection of weapons strapped to the belt.

"Who are you?" I said.

"Let me introduce myself. I'm Stoop," he said, reaching up to shake my hand, "and I've chosen you to be my apprentice."

"What kind of
apprentice?"

"The monster
hunting kind, of
course!" said Stoop.
"I've been hunting
monsters for two
hundred years now,
and that's quite
long enough. I want to put my feet up,
but I can't retire until I find someone suitable
to take my place. Them's the rules. That's
where you come in. I'm going to teach you all
I know."

"Why me?"

"There's not many boys who can kill
an Ogre single-handedly." Stoop nodded
appreciatively at the dead Ogre lying on what
was left of my home. "That was a neat bit of
work. In fact, I think it should go in the book."

"What book?"

"I was getting to that."

As if from nowhere, Stoop produced an old, black, leather-bound book and held it out for me to take.

The title on the front said:

Monster Hunting For Beginners

"Everything you'll ever need to know about being a monster hunter is in that book," he assured me.

"Everything?" I said doubtfully. "It says here it's only for beginners."

"Ah, that's the thing. It's for beginners now, but watch . . ."

Stoop took back the book, and the title on the front instantly changed to *Monster Hunting For Grumpy Men With Shaggy Beards, Red Noses And Battered Tin Helmets.*

"Hey, I'm not grumpy," he said.*

But you can't argue with a book. Especially not a magic one.

"You see, the book is whatever you need it to be," he continued. "Have it, it's yours. I'm giving it to you as a gift, out of the kindness of my heart. Do you want it?"

"Sure," I said, because I liked books.

I should have realised from the gleam of triumph in his eye as he handed it over that Stoop was up to something. But I was itching to open the book and see what was inside.

This was what the first page said.

* *Grumpily.*

For The Attention Of New Monster Hunters

No doubt you have lots of questions right now.
Questions like: What would happen if you untied
your belly button and yanked it really hard?

The answer to that one is: You'd unravel
in a big pile of blood and guts like spaghetti
bolognese.

A more important question is: What are
monster hunters, and what do they do?

Read carefully, because you're about to find
out. The truth is, new monster hunter, that there
are monsters everywhere, but only a few people
can see them, and an even smaller number are
~~unlucky~~ lucky enough to be picked as official
monster hunters. You are one of them.

Your job is to save the day when monsters start misbehaving. Which is most of the time. They are monsters, after all. How you deal with them depends on what kind of monsters they are. That's where this book comes in.

D is for Disappointed

Eagerly, I flicked through the pages.

Some of the monsters I recognised from stories, like Basilisks and Minotaurs and Gorgons. Others were less familiar.

There were Boggarts and Bogeys . . .

Galleytrots and Clabbernappers . . .

Slabberkins and Old Shocks . . .

As well as Incubusses and Succubusses and Doubledeckerbusses.

There was even one called the Crusted Hairy Snot Nibbler.

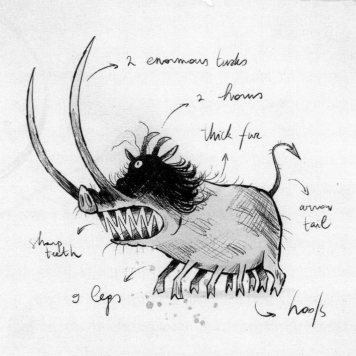

2 enormous tusks

2 horns

thick fur

arrow tail

sharp teeth

9 legs

hoofs

The Crusted Hairy Snot Nibbler

This particular monster is neither crusted, nor even that hairy. It also doesn't nibble snot as a general rule. Why would it? Snot is disgusting, and should never be used as a sandwich filling unless

the only alternative is gooseberry jam. Scholars
have long disagreed over how the Crusted Hairy
Snot Nibbler got its name. Some say it must
have been named by someone who simply didn't
understand the meaning of the words "crusted",
"hairy", "snot" and "nibble". Whatever the reason,
the Crusted Hairy Snot Nibbler actually looks like
a warthog with one eye, nine stumpy legs, and
tusks so long that they can pick up radio stations
on three continents. It is most commonly found in
wooded areas of Papua New Guinea, and is best
approached with caution, not to mention a peg on
the end of your nose.

"When you come across a new monster,"
Stoop explained, "you write up the details on
a blank page. That way the book stays up to
date. Here's one I added last week."

"Huge Warty Green Thingummy," I read

aloud. "Couldn't you think of a better name than that?"

"I was in a rush," said Stoop awkwardly. "What matters is writing down a description while the monster's fresh in your memory. That entry instantly appears in alphabetical order in all the other copies belonging to other monster hunters around the world. Look, there's a new entry appearing as we speak about an outbreak of Storm Fiends in Saskatchewan. Wherever that is."*

I watched the words forming on the page with growing excitement. Mum had been right all along. The world WAS full of monsters, and they were all in the pages of this **Admittedly Quite Peculiar** book.

There was only one thing I didn't understand.

"Why are there no dragons in here?" I said, turning to D and finding it empty of the creatures I'd always longed to see the most.

Stoop gave a scoff.

*It's in Canada, I looked it up.

"There's no such thing as dragons," he laughed. "Everybody knows that."

The excitement brewing inside me sizzled out like a hot coal dropped in a puddle. I hadn't been so disappointed since the night Dad wouldn't let me stay up late to watch a horror film in case it gave HIM nightmares.

"It doesn't matter anyway." I said, closing the book with a sigh and trying to hand it back to Stoop. "I can't run off to become a monster hunter. I have to find Dad first. I still have no idea where he's gone."*

"You can't change your mind now," Stoop said. "You've already agreed to take the job."

"No, I haven't."

"Yes, you have. I'll prove it," he said.

---

* The only thing I did know for sure is that it wasn't on a round-the-world voyage.

Cabbage and Custard

Stoop unhooked a magnifying glass from his belt so that I could read the faint spidery writing on the inside cover of the book.

Foolishly receiving this book as a gift constitutes formal acceptance of the job of monster hunter. Refusal to comply will result in some thoroughly nasty punishment involving custard. Unless you like custard. In which case we'll think of something else.

"Always read the small print," Stoop said with a grin. "That's one piece of advice I'll give you for nothing."

"You tricked me!" I said.

"I know," he grinned. "Clever, isn't it?"

I'd never felt so dumb.

"Cheer up," he said heartily. "Everyone falls for it. I did too, when I was your age. When you get tired of being a monster hunter, just find a suitable apprentice and trick them the same way I did with you. It's easy."

"It doesn't look like I have much choice, does it?"

I really hated custard, after all.

"Being a monster hunter isn't so bad," said Stoop. "The pay isn't great, and you are at constant risk of death, which tends to put people off for some weird reason. But you're your own boss, and you get to travel to exciting

and exotic places,
like Peru, China, the
Great Barrier Reef,
Birmingham . . .
Plus you get all the
boiled cabbage you
can eat."

I didn't have the heart to
tell him that I didn't like
cabbage either.*

Besides, what did
I have to lose?

Mum was dead.

Dad had vanished.

Everything I'd ever known had been buried
under ten tonnes of rubble.**

This was my chance to prove at last that I
wasn't just some weedy kid with glasses who
couldn't stick up for himself when it mattered,
but an apprentice monster hunter who had a
catapult and wasn't afraid to use it.

* Particularly when it was boiled.

** It might have been more, I'm just guessing.

With Stoop's help, I might even be able to find out what had really happened to Dad. His disappearance had to be connected with Aunt Prudence and the Ogre in some way.

That settled it.

"When do I start?" I said.

"Right away!"

Dressed for Success

The first thing we had to do, Stoop said, was get me kitted out in the correct gear. A monster hunter had to **Look The Part**.

"Let me see what I've got."

He opened his bag and started rummaging around inside. There was a lot of clanking as he threw out more and more weapons before he eventually produced a spare tin helmet, exactly the same as the one he was wearing.

It was also exactly the same size.

"Try this on."

"I don't think it'll fit," I said, not wanting to sound ungrateful.

"Wanna bet?" said Stoop with a grin.

Intrigued, I took the tin helmet and placed it on top of my head. Just as I expected, it sat there like a thimble on a giant ant hill.

"I told you it wouldn't –"

I stopped.

An extraordinary thing was happening.

The helmet was changing shape, stretching and moulding to fit my head.

Before I knew it, I was wearing a snug, new, slightly less battered tin helmet.

The same thing happened when I took off my jumper and tried on the leather tunic. At first it was like trying to squeeze a baby's sleep suit on to a St Bernard dog.*

Then it too morphed into exactly the right size and shape for my body.

The belt came next. One minute it looked no bigger than a liquorice lace. The next it unfurled like a snake waking up, and wrapped itself around my waist, with lots of hooks on

_____

* If you've never done that, do give it a go some day, it's hilarious.

46

which to hang weapons, though for now I only had my catapult. I'd need **Special Training** before I was allowed anything sharp, Stoop explained, otherwise I'd probably just chop off my own ears with the first swipe.

"There's not much point wasting time on lessons yet, though," he added, "because most apprentice monster hunters only last about six minutes before being munched. Six and a half, if they're really good at running."

"Was that another bit you forgot to mention?" I said.

"It slipped my mind," Stoop said slyly. "Don't worry, I'm sure that won't happen to you. You've got the knack for monster hunting, I can tell. Here, what do you think?"

He fished out a small mirror from his bag and held it up so that I could see my reflection.

I still looked like me. I was as small as ever, with glasses and a burst of wild hair, but there was something different about me too.

Something . . . special?

Stoop seemed satisfied with the result. Now that I looked right, he said it was time to move on to the Next Step, and that was to find out what the Ogre had been doing in my garden in the first place.

Ogres generally lived in the wild.

Most monsters did.

"We should check his pockets for clues," I suggested.

"See what I mean?" said Stoop. "You're going to be good at this job."

Unfortunately, I was about to discover that life as a monster hunter was never that simple.

The Ogre had gone.

The Rules

I might not have known much about monster hunting yet, but I felt as sure as anyone could be that Ogres weren't in the habit of getting up and walking away after being killed.

That's what Zomblings do.

This is what *Monster Hunting For Beginners* has to say about Zomblings.

Zomblings

You know what Zombies are, right? Well, Zomblings are exactly the same, except they look like babies. These fearsome creatures have existed in many

countries throughout history, but
they all have one thing in common.
They eat brains. They don't even
cook them first in a nice sauce
before serving them up with
chips. They eat them raw.
If you've only just met a
Zombling and are reading
this for advice about
what to do next, let's
put it simply: RUN!
Seriously, just run.
(If possible, away from
the Zomblings, and
not towards them.)

Better still, if you have
a friend who can't run
as fast as you, try to run
in the same direction as
them because the Zomblings
are bound to catch them first,

big eyes

long fingers

eats 7
brains a
week

then it'll be their brains being eaten and not yours. Having said all that, if you're still standing there, reading this book, then it may already be too late. Try not to worry about it. Many animals live perfectly happy lives without brains. Starfish, for example. And PE teachers.

"That is odd," said Stoop, staring at the spot where the Ogre had definitely been a few minutes earlier. "Are you sure he was dead?"

"I thought he was," I said, "but I didn't dare go any closer to check. I must have knocked him out instead. Poor thing. I'll bet he has a terrible headache now."

"It's better than being dead," pointed out Stoop reasonably. "You can get tablets at the chemist for a sore head. They haven't invented tablets for being dead yet. I must say, though, I am relieved he's still alive."

"You are?" I said in shock, because Stoop

didn't seem to be the sort of person who'd lose a night's sleep over a dead monster or two.*

"The thing is," he admitted, tugging his beard in embarrassment, "we're not actually allowed to kill monsters."

"What?"

"Don't get me wrong. We're permitted to use a **Reasonable Amount of Force** in self-defence or to protect innocent members of the public, but that doesn't include killing. That's one of the reasons I'm retiring. It's not as much fun as it used to be. I tried lopping off a few heads, but you wouldn't believe the fuss they made about it back at Monster Hunting HQ. I was filling out forms for a week."

"Would I have got into trouble if I had killed the Ogre?" I said.

"You're new, you didn't know any better. They'd probably have let you off with a warning."

"Is that what happened to you when you

* Or three.

killed the Anticore too?"

"The what?"

I took *Monster Hunting For Beginners* out of my pocket and turned to a bit near the front.

Anticore

Have you ever heard of the Manticore? It was a fearsome creature from ancient times, with a lion's body, a man's head, and the sting of a scorpion. Facing a monster with a lion's body and a man's head might sound slightly less scary than facing one with a man's body and a lion's head. Lions' teeth are designed to tear flesh to pieces, whereas human teeth are so feeble that even chewing toffee makes all their fillings fall out. The Manticore, though, had three rows of sharp iron teeth, which meant that it had no

trouble eating toffee at all, and even less trouble
eating monster hunters. The Anticore looks exactly
the same, except that it's no bigger than an ant.
Hence the name. Obviously.   Actual size.

"I'd forgotten about that one," Stoop said.
"It says here you defeated him in Fierce
Combat."
"Does it?"
I pointed to the relevant paragraph.

Anticores had not been seen in the wild for many
years until last Tuesday, when Stoop reported that
he'd defeated one in Fierce Combat after it resisted
all appeals to come quietly.

"See?"

"I may have exaggerated a bit," Stoop was forced to concede, face turning almost as red as his nose. "I actually stepped on him when I was running for a train. I wouldn't have noticed if it hadn't been for the squelch. But that was different. It was an accident. You can't kill monsters, and that's that."

"So what do you do with them?"

"We capture and rehabilitate them, then release them back into the wild once they've mended their ways. Whales and owls have protection, after all, so why not monsters?"

"Owls don't eat people," I said.*

"It's not my fault. I don't make the rules," said Stoop. "We can't kill them and that's that. It's forbidden under **Section 38 of the Endangered Monsters Act**."

That still didn't mean we could let this particular Ogre just stomp off in search of another meal. Aunt Prudence had had a

---

* *I was wrong about that. It's clearly stated in* Monster Hunting For Beginners *that the Outer Mongolian Dwarf Owl is notorious for swooping down and seizing lollipop men and women in the belief that they're actual lollipops.*

narrow escape. The next victim might not be so lucky.

We had to find him.

Fast.

But where would an Ogre with a sore head go once he came to his senses again?

X

Marks the Spot

"Do you think that sheet of paper flapping about in the rubble might be a clue?" I asked after we'd been considering the question of the Ogre's whereabouts for a little while.

"In my experience as a monster hunter, sheets of paper flapping about in rubble are almost always **Vital Clues**," Stoop said excitedly. "Go and get it before it blows away."

Hurrying over, I grabbed hold of it and pulled it from the wreckage.

Carefully, I began to unfold it – but not carefully enough. The piece of paper instantly

saw its chance to escape. It snatched hold of a passing edge of wind and made a break for it.

Stoop grabbed the sheet, but it yanked him off the ground, and he was left dangling in the air as if hanging from a badly-behaved parachute.

I grabbed his ankle just in time to rescue him from a new life as a bird.

With a loud

HARRUMPH, Stoop dropped back to earth, spreading the paper roughly on the ground, and sitting smack in the middle of it to stop it blowing away a second time.

The paper struggled a bit then lay still.

It knew when it was beaten.

Bending down to take a closer look, I saw that

the piece of paper was actually a map.

"The Ogre must have dropped it as he was making his getaway," I said. "Move over so that I can see it more clearly."

Stoop shuffled slightly to the left.

There, where he'd been sitting, was a cluster of houses, and a hill, and a wood, and a winding road, and a pair of crossed swords to show where a battle had been fought long ago.

"Now shuffle to the right."

Stoop protested, but did as he was asked.

This time I saw that there was some writing on the map – if you could call it writing. There were no words or letters, just blotches and splodges, as if a pen had caught a cold and sneezed ink all over the paper.

"It's gibberish," I said.

"That's where you're wrong," Stoop said. "It's not Gibberish. That's what Gibbers* speak. This is Ogrish. My Ogrish is like a bike that's been left out in the rain. Which is to say, it's a

---

* Gibbers are a bit like Waffs, only not so bloodthirsty. Having said that, Waffs are nowhere near as bloodthirsty as Scrots. Nothing is. Except for Tints. And Scruggs, but only during daylight hours.

bit rusty, but I think this is a map of somewhere called King's Nooze."

"King's Nooze?" I said. For some reason, the name sounded familiar. "Where's that?"

"Cornwall, according to the map."

"That's where Mum grew up!" I said, sure as I'd ever been about anything that it couldn't be a coincidence. "I've always wanted to go there, but Dad kept making excuses why we couldn't."

"If I know anything about dads, yours was probably just trying to stop you from getting eaten," Stoop said. "They have lots of trouble with monsters down there. That was Jack the Giant Killer's neck of the woods."

"Jack the who?" I said.

"Don't tell me you've never heard of Jack the Giant Killer!"

"Is he the same one as in Jack and the Beanstalk?" I said.

"No, this one's a different Jack. He just

happened to have the same name. Jack is a very common name for monster hunters. But I don't have to tell you that. You're one yourself now, Jack! This Jack was the most famous monster hunter of them all. He's the one who started this whole monster hunting business in the first place. He lived in King Arthur's time. Lucky for him, there were no rules back then about not killing monsters. He once tricked a wicked Giant into slicing open its own belly. Trust me, that's not easy to do."

"Do you really think King's Nooze is where the **Not Dead Ogre** was headed when he stopped off to eat Aunt Prudence then?" I said, as Stoop jumped smartly to his feet and folded away the map for safekeeping.

"I'd bet my life on it," he said. "Why else would there be directions to a place you've never even heard of flapping around in the ruins of your house? It must be his. We'd better hurry if we want to get there first, though. The

Ogre already has a head start."

"But Cornwall's miles away!" I protested.

"It'll take hours on foot."

"Want another bet?" said Stoop.

Not Too Big For My Boots

Stoop reached into his bag again.

This time he took out a pair of green boots.

Obviously, they were as tiny as his own, but I knew how it worked now. I pulled off my shoes, hoping I didn't have any holes in my socks, because it's always a bit embarrassing when that happens, and slipped the new boots on to the ends of my big toes.

They looked ridiculous dangling there, like mittens on an elephant . . . but not for long. Soon they'd enfolded themselves to fit my feet, as if they'd been made just for me.

They even had my name already stitched on the inside. That, said Stoop, was in case they were stolen while I was having a bath and I had to prove they were really mine.*

"These are seven league boots. All the best heroes in old stories owned a pair. Put these on and you can go seven leagues – that's about twenty-one miles, or 3,379,622.4 centimetres if you want to be silly about it – with every step. You can't be getting the bus when there's an emergency. I've been to Africa and back in a day in them."

"Don't people notice?"

"You move so fast all they see is a blur. That's where all the UFO sightings come from. It's monster hunters on their way to a job. Stand up and give them a go."

It was one small step for a monster hunter, but it was a giant leap for me.

Unfortunately, that giant leap ended with me upside down at the bottom of a tree.

* He said that happened more often than you'd think.

The next step took me to the top of the tree, where a bad-tempered squirrel started firing nuts at me from his secret store. I tried to reassure him that I wasn't about to steal his provisions, but neither of us understood one another's language, and Stoop was already calling on me to give the boots another go.

This time, I soared high over the garden wall and landed in the middle of the road.

Cars screeched to a halt, and drivers yelled at me to watch where I was going.

They soon shut up when Stoop, landing nimbly next to me, pulled out his dagger and threatened to pop their tyres.

"Hold on to my hand," said Stoop. "Magic boots take some getting used to."

Off we went, street by street at first, skipping across the tops of houses and churches, then in one bound we were in the next town, going faster and faster.

My head was spinning as fields and roads

and counties unfurled rapidly beneath us. We whizzed along so high off the ground that people down below looked like ants, and the ants didn't look like anything because they were too small to see.

In no time at all, apart from the time it took to get there, we were in King's Nooze.

Here Before?

There was something tinglingly familiar about King's Nooze. As I stood in the town square, looking round at the cobblestoned streets and higgledy-piggledy buildings, I almost felt as if I'd been here before.

There was a crooked clock tower that was telling a different time of day on each of its four faces, and all of them were wrong.

There was a butcher's, a baker's, and a candlestick maker's, though the baker sold nothing but candlesticks, and the candlestick maker sold nothing but cakes and buns.

As for the butcher's shop, that had been taken over by vegetarians and now stocked

nothing but carrots. There was also a flea market that sold actual fleas, and an old curiosity shop with a sign that said The Old Shop of Curious Things that was right next door to another called The New Shop Of Really Ordinary Stuff.

People were milling about, carrying placards that read ***Down With Monsters*** and ***Stop Eating Our Grannies***, and a man was standing on top of the stump of an old oak tree in the middle of the town square. He was wearing a top hat, and a gold chain around his neck, and he was shouting through a megaphone as a crowd chanted back.

"What do we want?"

"Not to be eaten!"

"When do we want it?"

"Every meal time, if at all possible!"

Stoop shook his head. "I fear, Jack, that we may be looking at a **Category Four** emergency here."

"Is that bad?"

"The best thing you can say about it is that it's not as bad as a **Category Five**. The book will explain."

I took out the *Monster Hunting For Beginners*. It fell open conveniently at the right page.

A Brief Note On Threat Levels

CATEGORY ONE: *The monsters are at it again, but no one has noticed, not even monster hunters. This one probably doesn't deserve a classification of its own, to be honest. It usually sorts itself out.*

CATEGORY TWO: *Monsters have done a fair bit of damage, but ordinary members of the public have yet to notice. If a monster hunter gets to the scene quickly enough, it's usually sufficient to contain the situation.*

CATEGORY THREE: One or two people have started to realise that there's a big, scary-looking creature in the vicinity where there was no big, scary-looking creature before. Your priority is to deal with the aforementioned big, scary-looking creature (or creatures) while reassuring the aforementioned person (or persons) that they're only seeing things.

CATEGORY FOUR: The monsters are misbehaving so badly that it's been noticed by far too many people to keep quiet. There may be outbreaks of dread, terror, screaming, pandemonium and other really annoying behaviour. Your job has now got much harder, but there's no extra pay so don't bother asking. The International Association of Monster Hunters isn't made of money, you know.

CATEGORY FIVE: Monsters have taken over the world, leading to the possible end of civilisation as we know it. This rarely happens. In fact, it never has, or you'd have heard about it. If it does happen, there's not much you can do to prevent it, so thank you for your service. Do try to have a nice death, and please file a full report afterwards for our official records.

Facing My Fears

"What are we going to do?" I said in alarm.

It didn't seem fair that my very first mission should be a **Category Four** emergency, rather than having the chance to get some practice by dealing with a few Twos and Threes first.

"What I'm going to do," said Stoop, "is nip off to the candlestick maker's to get myself something nice to eat. I'm famished. You'd better go and ask someone what's going on."

"Who should I ask?"

"Blowed if I know. What about her?"

Stoop nodded towards a girl who was

standing at the edge of the crowd. She was about the same age as me, but taller, because who isn't?

I couldn't breathe all of a sudden. What was Stoop thinking? Talking to strange girls was far scarier than facing monsters.

I was bound to go red.

I always did.

When I'd asked Dad about being shy, he simply told me not to worry about it, because worrying only makes things worse. If anything, that made me feel more anxious than before, because it got me worried about worrying, and there's nothing more worrying than that.

The problem is that he's not very good at giving advice. Mum would have known what to say, but she wasn't here, was she?

The most helpful thing Dad could think to tell me was that girls were just the same as boys, except that girls don't find burping as funny. That wasn't very helpful either, because who doesn't find burping funny?

There was only one thing for it.

I had to **Face My Fears**.

I took a deep breath, walked up to the girl and coughed to get her attention.

"Hello," I said, hoping my voice didn't sound too squeaky. It often did when I was nervous. I hated having to read my work aloud in class. I'd rather be hung upside down from a washing line and poked with cactus plants.*

"Hello yourself," she said, turning round and giggling as she let out a huge burp. It cheered me up no end to know that girls did find burping funny, whatever Dad might say.

I was also glad to see that she was wearing glasses too. In my experience, all the friendliest people do.

"I like your boots," she said.

"Thanks," I said. "I'm Jack."

* Not really, but you get the point.**
** Literally, if you are unlucky enough to get poked by a cactus.

"I'm Nancy."

I was amazed.

Not because she was called Nancy, which was a perfectly good name, and still is, and certainly not because she liked my boots, because why wouldn't she? I liked them too.

It was what she said next that took me aback.

"They're seven league boots, aren't they?"

Nancy Tells All

I could tell at once that Nancy was **No Ordinary Girl**. The children at school would have sniggered if I'd told them I had a pair of magic boots.* Nancy could tell what they were just by looking at them.

"Don't be so astonished," she said with a laugh as my mouth fell open but no words came out. "I've always been mad about magic. The children at my old school didn't believe me when I said that it was real. That's why Mum and I moved to King's Nooze a while ago, because it seemed like the sort of place where anything could happen. Now it has!"

"Is that what everyone's angry about?" I

---

* If they were feeling particularly spiteful, they might even have guffawed.

said as another shout rose from the crowd.

Nancy nodded, and pointed past the crooked clock tower to a green hill that towered over the town. That, I thought, must be the hill I'd seen on the map.

"An Ogre made his home up there about a week ago," Nancy said. "Every day he comes down that path, picks up two or three locals, then takes them back to grind their bones and make his bread. You know, like in the stories? I'll say one thing for that Ogre, he's a stickler for tradition. He's been told repeatedly that it's against food safety regulations, but he insists that's how it's always been and he's not changing his ways for anyone. He says it adds some crunch to his sandwiches."

"I'll bet it does."

"No one minded to begin with," she went on, the words tumbling fast from her lips, "because it meant there was less of a queue at the corner shop, but it's getting out of hand. He's not content with three meals a day like any normal respectable Ogre. He keeps popping in without warning for elevenses, twelveses, halfpastoneoclockses, and all the snacks inbetween. The shopkeepers say it's ruining the passing trade. King's Nooze is usually full of visitors at this time of year."

"Why hasn't anyone sent for a monster hunter to get rid of the Ogre?" butted in Stoop, returning from the candlestick maker's shop with a large bag of jam tarts and rubbing roughly at all the crumbs that were now trapped in his beard like flies in a spider's web. "I'd know about it if they had. Any requests for assistance that come into the HQ of the International League of Monster Hunters in Llanfairpwllgwyngyllgogerychwyrndrobwllllantysiliogogogoch* are instantly passed on to all authorised personnel by carrier penguin."

"Don't you mean pigeon?" said Nancy.

"I know what I mean," said Stoop. "That's

* That's a town in Wales. The name is Welsh for "town with a very long and silly name that's nowhere near as the silly as the people who named it."

how I heard about the Ogre in Jack's garden, because a woman across the street complained that he'd trodden on her rhododendrons. The Ogre, that is, not Jack. It had all the makings of a **Category Three** emergency until Jack stepped in and dealt with the Ogre himself."

"I can see there's more to you than meets the eye, Jack," said Nancy, looking at me with new respect. "Is that why you're here now? To get rid of the Ogre? If so, you haven't come a moment too soon. The truth is that nobody knows what to do. They've never encountered a monster before. I told the Mayor – he's the one in the top hat and gold chain, in case you hadn't guessed – that he should send for help immediately, and he promised to write to the Appropriate Authorities as soon as he could find his favourite fountain pen."

"A likely excuse!" said Stoop.

"Don't blame me. I'm not in charge. Why don't you go and ask him yourself?"

"I will!" said Stoop . . . but he didn't.

He never got the chance.

I put a finger to my lips.

"Can you feel that?" I whispered as the ground started to tremble under our feet and a shadow fell across the square.

I knew what that meant.

The Ogre was coming down the hill.

The Ogre
Helps Himself

The bell in the crooked clock tower
BOOMED in unison with the sound of
approaching footsteps. For the first time ever,
it was telling the right time, and that was the
time to scarper.

"Run!"

"Hide!" everybody cried.

They all dropped their placards and bolted
for the nearest house, with the Mayor at the
head of the pack. He insisted that he was
leading them to safety, but he knocked over
at least nine people on the way, all the while
yelling: "Take the children! Take the children! I
hear they're delicious!"

Doors slammed shut.

Curtains closed.

Soon only the three of us were left in the square. We hid behind the oak tree stump, and watched as the Ogre stomped into view.

The Ogre in my garden had been wearing clothes. Very tight clothes that looked as if they might burst at any moment from the strain of holding in so much Ogre, but clothes all the same. This Ogre was not only bigger, he'd also forgotten to put on his pants.

That was my first glimpse of a monster's rear end, and I couldn't help hoping it would be my last. It wasn't a pretty sight.

I could only stare as he paused to sniff the air before tearing the roof off the nearest shop and lifting out the candlestick maker as she was in the middle of removing a tray of freshly baked hot cross buns out of the oven.

"Bother," growled the Ogre, realising that he had no pockets in which to carry his meal.

He contented himself with
unroofing the shop next
door and picking up the
baker in the other hand.
The baker tried to defend
herself with some of the
candlesticks she'd been
making that morning, but
it was no good. Candlesticks
are no defence against
monsters.

Satisfied, the Ogre
turned on his heels and
headed back up the hill,
humming to himself as
he went: "**Fee Fi
Fo Fum**."*

Slowly all the
townsfolk emerged
from their hiding places,
muttering how glad they

* *Actually he was humming "Fo Fum
Fi Fee" because he didn't know the right
words, but it's the thought that counts.*

were that it was the baker and the candlestick maker who'd been taken instead of them, because no one really needed that many candlesticks and the candlestick maker charged far too much for birthday cakes, and always skimped on the icing sugar too.

"She didn't put enough jam in the jam tarts either!" shouted Stoop, joining in.

"Fear not, terrified townsfolk!" exclaimed Nancy, hopping on to the stump of the oak tree and waving for attention. "Help is at hand. This is Jack. He's a monster hunter. He's come to King's Nooze to kill the Ogre!"

"Actually, Nancy, we're not allowed to . . ." I tried to explain, but I was quickly surrounded by people demanding to know what I intended to do to save them, because two portions wouldn't fill up the Ogre for long.

He'd soon be back for more.

"Well?" they said expectantly, glaring down at me. "What's your great plan, Jack?"

Out of Hand

I clambered on to the stump next to Nancy to avoid the crush, trying hastily to think of a plan.

I always felt awkward when too many people were staring at me.

"What we need to do," I began, "is . . . that is to say, I think it might be a good idea to . . . or maybe . . . given the circumstances . . . we could . . ."

It was hopeless. Every thought I'd ever had was trickling from my head like lemonade from a leaky bucket.*

I hadn't needed a plan when the Ogre grabbed Aunt Prudence. I'd simply grabbed the catapult without thinking and let the rock do the talking.

---

* Assuming that's where you chose to store your lemonade, and it's nobody else's business if you do.

It was more complicated now that there were rules to being a monster hunter and everyone was relying on me. What would *Monster Hunting For Beginners* say?

That was it!

Stoop had reassured me that everything I'd ever need to know was in that book. There was no better moment to prove it. I took it out, hoping it wouldn't take too long to find the answer. The crowd was growing restless.

"We haven't got all day, you know," someone shouted from the back.

"I have," said someone else.

"Me too," said another.

"You keep out of this," the first voice retorted.

"Don't you tell me what to do!"

"I'll tell you what I like!"

"Please," I said, "don't fight."

It was no use. Things were getting out of hand. Soon there'd be fisticuffs.

"Wait a second," said the Mayor.

He'd finally come out of hiding once he was certain that the Ogre had gone, and he was currently standing below me, squinting up at the title on the front of the book with barely disguised contempt.

"You're not even a fully qualified monster hunter?" he said. "You're just a BEGINNER?"

The townsfolk stopped squabbling with one another and turned on me instead.

"Everyone has to start somewhere,"I said.

I might as well have been speaking Actual Gibberish for all the notice they took of me.

Outraged, Stoop elbowed his way to the front of the crowd to confront the Mayor.

"We haven't come all this way to stand around here yackety-yacking," he said. "Do you want our help with your Ogre or not?"

"What business is it of yours, may I ask?" the Mayor replied, squinting down at Stoop from under the brim of his hat.

"For your information," said Stoop, "I happen

to be a fully qualified monster hunter, and Jack is my new apprentice, so if an Ogre rampaging round town isn't our business, then I'd like to know whose it is."

The Mayor snorted scornfully.*

"Not very big, are you?" he said.

"Not very big?" said Stoop indignantly. "I'll have you know that I won a silver medal at the Monster Hunting Games. I'd have got gold if it hadn't have been for this Swedish woman with pigtails who held the world record in Rounding Up Changelings."

They took no notice of him either.

One by one, the crowd began to drift away, shaking their heads, as the Mayor promised to order in some "proper monster hunters" at the earliest opportunity with no expense spared.

"What did I tell you?" said Stoop. "Some people just aren't worth saving."

"Don't listen to them, Jack," said Nancy, as I watched them go, feeling that I'd let everyone

*It's impossible to snort any other way.

91

down. "I'm sure you'll do a good job."

"You are?" I said.

"Of course. You've already killed one Ogre. Another one should be a piece of cake."

Stoop and I exchanged awkward glances.

"Do you want to tell her the bad news, or shall I?" he whispered.

Onwards and Upwards

We might not be allowed to kill monsters, but we couldn't just abandon the baker and the candlestick maker to their gruesome fate.

I insisted that we climb the hill Without Further Delay to rescue them, assuming that they hadn't already been eaten because then there wouldn't have been much left to rescue.

"Why don't you come with us?" I said to Nancy, who seemed like a girl who'd be good to have on our side if trouble broke out.

"Try stopping me!" she declared. "King's Nooze is my town now. I have a duty to protect it from all perils, dangers and threats."

"Shouldn't you tell your mum and dad where

you're going?" I asked.

There was no way Dad would have let me run off to fight an Ogre with two strange monster hunters I'd only met minutes ago.

He wouldn't even have let me run off to play with two kittens, just in case I pricked my finger on their whiskers.

"I can't tell Dad. He's dead," said Nancy matter-of-factly. "As for Mum, she's out of town on business today, but she trusts me to look after myself. She always says that you never know what's going to happen in life, so you might as well do what you really want to do, even if it's a bit scary, rather than sitting around miserably wishing that you had."

"That's a good motto," I acknowledged, thinking how I'd always wanted to have an adventure, and now here I was having one, and wishing that Dad had felt the same way, so we could have had an adventure together.

I took the opportunity as we set off up the

hill to fill her in about all the things that had happened since the day I came home from school a week ago to find Dad missing.

Telling her about Mum was easier than it usually was with other people. If anyone could understand how it felt, it was her.

She agreed that Dad's disappearance must have something to do with the Ogre who'd tried to eat Aunt Prudence in my garden that morning, and that in turn, Nancy said, had to be related to the Ogre in King's Nooze, because the unexpected appearance of TWO Ogres would be TOO much of a coincidence otherwise.

That made me all the more determined to press on and see where this latest line of investigation led us, but the climb was taking much longer than it should have done.

The candlestick maker had helpfully dropped a large quantity of hot cross buns to mark the way, like Hansel and Gretel in the fairy tale, and Stoop, less helpfully, was insisting on stopping

to eat every single one.*

Consequently, there was no sign of the baker or the candlestick maker when we finally did reach the top of the hill, and none of Dad either. Though now that I thought about it, expecting him to just be sitting there might've been asking too much.

What I did see was the entrance to a cave. Before it stood a blazing fire, with a huge cooking pot plonked down on the flames.

The Ogre – who by now had put on some

---

* The jam tarts, he explained, had only been to build up his appetite.

pants, sparing me from a second sight of his lumpy buttocks – had his back to us as he stirred the steaming contents of the pot.

I dreaded to think what, or who, might be in there, but I had to admit that it smelled quite good.

In fact, the aroma was so delicious that it would have made a Giant Fartdoodle's mouth water – and they don't even have mouths, according to *Monster Hunting For Beginners*.

Look it up if you don't believe me.

Giant Fartdoodles

These particular monsters are so called because they're big, they like farting, and they're also quite fond of doodling, preferably while farting at the same time. The main thing to bear in mind is that they have no mouths. How do Giant Fartdoodles eat if they have no mouths? Don't ask. Seriously. It'll put you right off your dinner. Didn't you hear me? I said don't ask. I won't warn you again. Look, if you must know, they eat with their bums. There, are you happy now? I told you it was best not to know.

Any Ideas?

We crouched down out of sight of the pot-stirring Ogre to plan our next move.

"If only we didn't have to capture him," sighed Nancy, who still couldn't believe that it was forbidden to kill monsters.

She had a point. This would have been the perfect opportunity to sneak up behind him and launch a surprise attack.

"Couldn't we roll this boulder on top of him and pretend it was an accident?" I said.

"It might start a landslide," said Stoop. "King's Nooze would be crushed. Why go to the trouble of saving people from an Ogre if they all end up flattened anyway?"

No one was getting flattened if she could help it, declared Nancy. The townsfolk might be silly, but they didn't deserve that.

"Landslides wouldn't hurt an Ogre anyway," Stoop added. "They love being bashed about with rocks. Have you ever watched a building being demolished by a wrecking ball swinging from a chain?"

"Yes."

"Look closer next time. It's usually an Ogre dangling on the end of the chain. That's what lots of them do after they've been returned to the community. They work in the construction industry bashing down walls."

"If they're so tough," I said, "how did I manage to knock one out with a single stone?"

Stoop shrugged.

"Dunno," he said. "Lucky shot, I guess."

"It wasn't lucky for the Ogre," said Nancy.

"I've got a suggestion," I said, still unsure how anyone was meant to protect the world from savage monsters when we weren't allowed to give them so much as a scraped elbow. "What about digging a pit, filling it with spikes . . . sorry, I mean really comfy cushions . . . then waiting for him to fall in?"

"Can't," said Stoop.

"Why not?"

"We haven't got a shovel. Or spikes, I mean comfy cushions."

"How about tying a blindfold on him so he can't see where he's going, then luring him to the nearest cliff?" interjected Nancy.

"Nice one," I said, imagining the satisfying SPLASH as the Ogre fell into the sea.

"That used to be one of my favourite methods in the old days," said Stoop wistfully, "but we're not allowed to do that any more either. The monsters all complained that it was cheating. They hate it when you tie their shoelaces together as well. That's why most monsters wear slippers these days."

What we really needed at that moment was detachable heads, so that we could turn them upside down to see what fresh thoughts tumbled out, the same way you do with shoes when shaking out loose stones.

"Try the book," advised Nancy.

"It's not big enough to knock him out."

"I mean, look inside and see what it says."

"Of course! Why didn't I think of that?"

What Would Jack Do?

I got out my copy of *Monster Hunting For Beginners* and flipped to the right page.

Top 100 Ways To Defeat An Ogre

ONE: *Say It With Dynamite.*

"That's no good," said Nancy. "As Stoop keeps reminding us, killing's not allowed, and dynamite doesn't tickle."

THIRTEEN: *Skewer the big clunking nuisance on the nearest available spike like a kebab.*

THIRTY-NINE: *Trick it into going for a swim inside a bubbling vat of acid.*

SIXTY FIVE: *Hire a helicopter and drop a second Ogre on top of the target. The ensuing scrap's sure to cause at least one death.*

"This is hopeless," I said. "We're not allowed to do any of these things."

"That's where you're wrong," said Nancy, who'd carried on reading the list.

She pointed a finger at the last suggestion.

ONE HUNDRED: *If for some odd reason slaughtering your Ogre isn't an option, there is one other method which might work, but it isn't half as much fun as the first ninety nine. (See Jack and the Beanstalk for details.)*

Jack and the Beanstalk was one of the stories that Mum always used to tell me when I was little. I'd heard it so often that I'd eventually asked her to please, please, please read me a different tale, even if it was one of those really soppy stories that teachers all seem to love with messages about how it's important to Be Kind or Never Tell Lies or Think Of Other People Before Yourself.*

As hurriedly as I could, I tried to remember the story of that other boy called Jack who sold a cow in return for some special beans

*I'm not saying you should be deliberately unkind, or tell fibs, or only think of yourself, but there's no need to go on about it.

that grew overnight into a huge beanstalk that rose to the sky, and how he climbed up it to a Giant's castle in the clouds, and stole a bag of gold coins, a hen that laid golden eggs, and –

"A magic harp!" I declared in triumph. "The Jack in that story used a magic harp to put the Giant to sleep."

I snapped the book shut.

"I don't suppose either of you have a magic harp, do you?" I asked my companions.

"Afraid not," said Nancy.

"Me neither," said Stoop.

"I do . . ." said a deep voice behind us.

Three Become Four

With a gulp – or rather three gulps, one for each of us – we turned round slowly, expecting to find that the Ogre had crept up behind us in his slippers when we weren't looking.

Instead, sitting a few feet away, looking glum, was a brown bear.

"Keep your curlers on," said the bear, rolling his eyes as we all froze in fear like peas in a freezer. "I'm not going to bite you. Why does everyone always think I want to bite them?"

"Because you have big teeth?" suggested Stoop.

"You have a big nose," said the bear, "but

that doesn't mean you're going to sniff me to death, does it?"

"I suppose not," said Stoop.

"You suppose right," the bear continued. "Think about it. Why would I want to fight you three when I could be getting my own back on Boffin instead?"

"Who's Boffin?" said Nancy.

"The Giant down there."

"It's an Ogre actually," I pointed out.

"What's the difference?" asked the bear.

"Well, a Giant is sort of . . . whereas an Ogre is more . . ."

I trailed off and

looked to Stoop for help.

"Giants aren't as stupid," Stoop said bluntly.
"They're also allergic to the colour blue,
and they can only change size and shape on
Sundays, whereas Ogres can do it all the time,
they just can't be bothered."

"What about Trolls?" said Nancy.

"I haven't got time to stand around all
day talking about the differences between
monsters!" Stoop cried. "Trolls turn to stone in
direct sunlight! There, are you happy now?"

"Well, I'll be glad to see the back of them,
whatever they are," the bear sighed heavily.
"That's my cave they've been living in since
they turfed me out last week."

I was about to sympathise, when I realised
what he'd said.

"Did you say . . . they?" I asked.

"You didn't think there was only one, did
you?" the bear said in disbelief. "I counted
seven, but bears can only count to seven so

there might be more. I wouldn't know."

"Show us," said Stoop.

The bear – whose name was Humbert,
he explained on the way, since no one had
bothered to ask, not that he wanted to make
a big thing about it, but it was generally
considered a Polite Thing to do on first meeting
– led us round the hill.

There was the side door, hidden behind a
bush to confuse burglars.*

As soon as we slipped inside, a foul stench hit
my nose, but I didn't want to mention it in case
that was how bears' caves are meant to smell.
I'd never been in one before, and I didn't want
to hurt Humbert's feelings.

It wasn't long before I discovered what was
REALLY making that dreadful smell.

*Why the burglars couldn't get in through the front of the cave, where
there was no door at all, just a big hole, I don't know. Maybe they
liked a challenge.

In the Cave

"Get a whiff of those brutes," whispered Stoop. "Haven't they heard of soap?"

Humbert was right – Boffin was about as alone as a duck-billed platypus who's invited all his duck-billed platypus pen pals to come and stay for a Duck-Billed Platypus Pen Pals Only weekend.

The floor of the cave was piled high with sleeping Ogres. They slept on the floor. They snoozed in corners. They sprawled on each other like coats on a bed at a party.

Some had tusks. Some had horns. Some had tusks that looked like horns, and one had a horn that looked like the Tower of London.

Another had no horn at all, because he didn't have a head and there was nowhere for it to grow. He must have saved a fortune on hats.

There were definitely more than seven.

There were more than thirteen.

In fact, there were so many that, if I had to guess the right number, I would've said it was somewhere between "Yikes, get me out of here!" and "DIDN'T YOU HEAR WHAT I SAID THE FIRST TIME?"

"They said the only reason they didn't eat me is because I'm too furry," said Humbert.

"No one likes hairy food," agreed Stoop.

"So they let me go," said the bear. "But now I have nowhere to sleep, and the rent's due on Monday. What am I going to do?"

I had to admit that was a **Very Good Question**. But before I could think of a **Very Good Answer**, Humbert suddenly clamped his paws over his ears as if he'd heard a rude word.

He hadn't, but it's just as well that he did cover his ears, because right then lots of rude words really did burst out of Stoop in response to a deafening noise which was filling the air . . .

WHAT ON EARTH WAS THAT HULLABALOO?

Hullabaloo

If you ever think of looking for a Hullabaloo, the best advice would be: Think again. Only ten monster hunters have ever met one, and nine didn't live to tell the tale. The one who did survive spent the next six months hiding under the bed, and it wasn't even her own bed, and all she could say was "Cripes!" and "Jeepers!" and "You've got to be kidding me!" When she eventually recovered, she drew the only known picture of a Hullabaloo, revealing it to be a goat-like beast whose glance is so fearsome that it can turn pebbles into stones, but, because pebbles already are stones, no one ever notices. They can also turn six eggs into an omelette, but anybody can do that if they have a frying pan and a dab of butter, so it isn't that impressive. I realise this doesn't sound very spine-chilling, but the statistics speak for themselves. Don't mess with Hullabaloos.

Tiptoes And Tip-Paws

To be clear, it wasn't a Hullabaloo.
These are Hullabaloos . . .

Our hullabaloo was a loud clanging noise, not
a monster. It felt like being hit repeatedly on the
head with a large cooking pot.

Or so I imagined, never having been struck
with a pot of any kind.*

The clanging came from a large gong.

Boffin was banging it to let the other Ogres
know that lunch was ready.

Gradually they started waking up, scratching
themselves and breaking wind, before

---

* *Aunt Prudence once tossed a cereal bowl at me when I had the cheek to
wish her a Good Morning when she wasn't expecting it, but I managed
to dodge out of the way before it connected with my skull.*

117

lumbering outside to dunk their heads in the stew and **SLURP** it straight from the pot.

They had the worst table manners I'd ever seen, and that's really saying something, because I was once made to sit next to Stanley Jenkins at lunch and everyone knows how off-putting it is watching him eat a tuna roll.

Now that they were gone, I could see what a mess the Ogres had made of Humbert's home. His four-poster bed had turned into a no-poster bed and the mattress was covered with green stains like the beach when the tide goes out but is too lazy to take the seaweed with it.*

There was also mud all over Humbert's nice carpet, and there were so many springs poking untidily out of his favourite armchair that it looked as if a man with curly metal hair was climbing out of it from the inside.

"This all very peculiar," said Stoop. "Ogres hate sharing food. They hate it more than having a bath and putting on clean underwear.

I couldn't say what they were, but suspected they had recently been up the Ogres' noses.

This must be an AGM."

"An agey what?" asked Humbert.

"It stands for **Abominable General Meeting**," said Stoop. "That's what it's called when monsters get together to plan some extra special trouble. Mischief doesn't make itself, you know. Lots of monsters have one. Last week it was the Patagonian Killer Bees. Their plan was to all start humming the same song until it got into people's heads, then they'd not be able to stop humming it too, even if they hated the tune, and they wouldn't know why they were doing it. The bees said it would drive everyone mad."

"How did you stop them?"

"I didn't," said Stoop. "It's going to be a very annoying summer."

"It isn't what they're doing that matters, but stopping them from doing it," said Nancy, "and for that we need a certain magic harp, in case you've forgotten. Don't you think we ought to be looking for it and then Getting Out Of Here before the Ogres come back?"

"Nancy's right," I said, and Nancy wholeheartedly agreed that she was.

Humbert led us on tiptoes – or tip-paws, in his case – to a cupboard at the back of the cave where he'd kept the magic harp ever since ordering it last winter from a catalogue.

He opened the door.

The good news was that he immediately found his knitting bag, which he'd been forced to leave behind when the Ogres kicked him out. That had been a great pity at the time, he explained, because he'd nearly finished a new pair of extra woolly socks.*

The bad news was that the harp wasn't there.

---

* Bears get through socks at a terribly fast rate on account of their sharp claws.

No Way Out

"It'll turn up," said Humbert, refusing to give up hope. "Nothing's ever lost for ever."

"Not even people?" I said.

"Especially not people," the bear replied, laying a huge paw on my shoulder. "They're always with you as long as you remember them."

"Right now I'd rather you remembered where the ruddy harp is," Stoop snarled.

I tried to take comfort from Humbert's words, but that wasn't easy just then, because, while we'd been standing there talking, the Ogres had finished eating and were trooping noisily back into the cave. The way to the side door was now blocked, and there was no use hiding. Ogres might be stupid, but they do have a strong sense of smell. The only reason they hadn't spotted us yet is because they were belching in each other's faces to see who had the stinkiest breath.*

"What are we going to do?" said Nancy, as we pressed ourselves hard against the wall.

I didn't know the answer to that.

What I did know was that this was my first mission as an official monster hunter, and I wasn't ready to give up yet.

There had to be a way to get help.

There was!

I looked up HELP under H in *Monster Hunting For Beginners.*

Fortunately, the words shone faintly like glow worms, because a monster hunter can't always expect to have a torch to hand.

Unfortunately, all it said was this . . .

---

* *This is a traditional after dinner game among Ogres, and, to be fair, it is quite fun.*

Help!

An expression that is traditionally uttered loudly when in the presence of monsters.

I didn't need reminding of that. Since being tricked into becoming Stoop's apprentice, "Help!" had practically been my middle name.

I was about to shut the book in despair when I saw a blob of what looked like marmalade* at the bottom of the page. I wiped it off with the edge of my thumb to see what was written underneath.

When all else seems lost in a sticky situation, try looking for a secret door or tunnel. There usually is one somewhere.

That was more like it.

---

* *I didn't taste it to be sure, because it's hard to think of anything more disgusting than marmalade. No, wait. I just thought of something FAR more disgusting. And smellier. Thankfully, it wasn't that either. .*

I held out the book at arm's length so that the light fell on the wall.

"What are you doing?" hissed Stoop. "They're going to see us!"

"They already have," said Nancy.

The Ogres were no longer sniffing each other's burpy breath. They were turning towards the light with puzzled expressions, as if they'd just been asked a really difficult question, such as: "What's one plus one?"

"We're done for!" said Stoop.

"Not if we crawl through there," I said.

The light was dim, but it shone just enough to reveal a hole in the wall.

Humbert insisted that the hole hadn't been there when he lived in the cave.

It was just another example of the damage that had been done to his home, but at that moment it was our only hope of escape.

I stuck my head into the hole to see what my eyes could make out. I soon discovered that what they could make out was . . . nothing.

I turned round to ask everyone if they thought it was safe to climb inside, only to realise the time for **Discussing Our Options** was past. The Ogres had finally picked up our scent and were stomping through the cave in our direction. I thought it was unlikely that they wanted to thank us for dropping in.

"Jump!" said Stoop.

Before I could point out the dangers of leaping into mysterious holes without knowing what might be lurking inside them, he shoved me hard in the back, and I found myself hurtling head first into empty air.

Nancy grabbed hold of my hand as I fell forward, and Stoop grabbed hold of her foot, and Humbert grabbed hold of Stoop's boot, and together we all tumbled untidily through the gap in the wall with a loud collective

"AAAAARRGGGHHH!"

Down we went into black nothingness, down, down, down, and I wondered if this was the moment that my adventure would finally come to the **Grimmest Of Grim Ends . . .**

Going Underground

It wasn't. I wouldn't have been around to tell the tale if that had been The End.

One thing I've learned from being a monster hunter is that it doesn't matter how deep a hole might be, if you fall down it long enough you will eventually reach the . . .

BOTTOM!

The only question is how much it's going to hurt when you get there.

The answer in this case, I was pleased to discover, was **Not Very Much**.

That's because Nancy and I landed on Humbert, who was softer than a bouncy castle.

Humbert wasn't harmed either. It takes more than falling down a hole to bruise a bear.

Stoop wasn't so lucky. He'd reached the

ground first for some weird reason, and Humbert had promptly landed on top of him.

The bear immediately rolled off him with a heartfelt apology, and helped Stoop to his feet again, as the man muttered that retirement couldn't come soon enough.

"I think we're in a tunnel," I said as my eyes adjusted to the gloom.

"You don't say?" muttered Stoop, who still hadn't forgiven us all for squashing him.

"A tunnel has to lead somewhere," said Nancy encouragingly, trying to take Stoop's mind off his aches and pains, "and that somewhere might be a way out. I say we follow it and see where it leads."

Without waiting for anyone else's opinion, she set off at a trot into the darkness

We had no choice but to follow her.

Soon we were trooping through one dark tunnel after another in single file, with Nancy at the front, Stoop and me behind, and Humbert at the back. The bear took a ball of wool from his knitting bag and let it unwind behind us so we'd be able to find the way back if needed.

There was so little light down here that it wouldn't have made any difference if we'd closed our eyes. After a while, even opening up *Monster Hunting For Beginners* didn't help.

Deeper and deeper we went into the dark, until we were bumping into each other's noses and elbows, and banging our heads on the low, knobbly roof, and treading on various toes, which didn't improve Stoop's bad temper one bit.*

The tunnel didn't make things easier. It twisted like an old rubber band, sometimes splitting off into other tunnels, just to confuse us. Each time we came to a new branch, we stopped to discuss whether to go left or right.

Humbert's nose sniffed out the freshest air, and that was the way we chose. Sometimes it led to a dead end, and Stoop grumbled. Sometimes it brought us right back to where we'd started, and

I was beginning to realise that very few things did.

Stoop grumbled at that too.

He also grumbled when it seemed that we were heading in the right direction.

Stoop just liked grumbling.

I began to wonder if we'd ever get out of there, and what would happen if we didn't.

I'd never see Dad again, and Nancy would never see her mum, and neither of them would ever know what had happened to us.

There'd also be no one to warn people in King's Nooze that there wasn't only one Ogre up here, but a whole team of them, and that they probably weren't here to play Ludo.

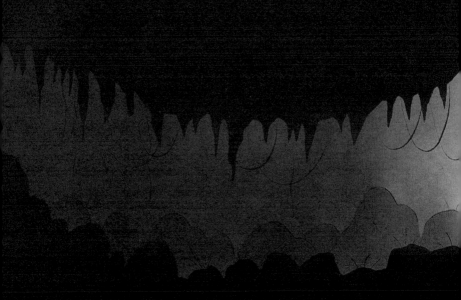

"You do have some gloomy thoughts sometimes, don't you?" said Nancy.

"Can you hear what I'm thinking?" I said.

"No, but it's darker than the inside of an acorn down here and you haven't said anything for ages. I guessed you must be **Getting Downhearted**."

"Aren't you?"

"Not in the slightest," she said, pointing. "Look, there's a light up ahead."

Could we really have found a way out?

The Mystery Deepens

Expecting the worst, I inched forward and peeped round the corner. Sure enough, there was another tunnel leading to daylight, but to get there we had to pass through another cave.

Unlike Humbert's cave, this one was mostly empty save for a huge armchair, and a table next to it on which stood a large bottle filled with a bright green liquid. The only other item of furniture was a cage, positioned in such a way that any sitting Ogre could watch it as if it was their favourite TV show.

Inside sat the baker and the candlestick maker, sharing the last of the hot cross buns.

I could have cheered.

They hadn't been in the stew, after all!

Happier still, they weren't alone. There were at least thirty other people locked in the cage with them. This must be all the townsfolk that Boffin had snatched on his various shopping trips down the hill.

What was going on? First the Ogres had all gathered in the cave at the top of the hill for some unknown reason. Then the townsfolk had been snatched one by one from their homes . . . but they hadn't been eaten.

Instead Boffin had brought them down here and locked them in a dungeon.

I shook my head. There was a time and a place for pondering what the Ogres were up to, and this wasn't it.

The Ogre who'd been keeping an eye on the prisoners might come back at any moment.

Leaving Stoop and Humbert to keep an eye out for trouble – or better still, all four of their eyes – Nancy and I edged towards the cage, knocking gently on the bars to get the prisoners' attention. (I couldn't help being disappointed that Dad wasn't among them. There'd been a faint hope in my mind that he might be.)

Instantly they jumped to their feet and all started talking at once, demanding to know why it had taken so long to be rescued.

"You have to be quiet," I whispered, "while we think of a way to get you out."

"Use the key," said the baker.

"What key?"

"Which one do you think? The key hanging on the wall next to the fire, of course," chipped in the candlestick maker, as if I should have known that already.

I must admit that I hadn't expected them to be so cheeky. I was learning fast that people aren't always as grateful to be saved from monsters as you might expect.

I ran to the fireside.

There hung the key. All I had to do was reach out and take it . . .

"No, Jack!" yelled Nancy.

The warning came too late.

"OOOOOWWWW!"

Another Bop

I'd forgotten that metal keys get very hot when left too close to roaring flames.

As I juggled it from hand to hand to cool it down, wishing that I was wearing oven gloves, I quickly discovered that a few scorched fingers was the least of my problems.

"Help! Help!" the key cried in a high whiny voice. Which was strange, when I thought about it, because – like the Giant Fartdoodle – it didn't have a mouth.*

"He doesn't know magic keys can talk!" the baker said, as all the townsfolk laughed. I felt my cheeks going red with embarrassment.

What was wrong with them? Did they like

---

*It also didn't have a nose, or eyebrows, but you probably know that if you've ever seen a key before.

being locked up by monsters?

Their jeers soon turned to cries of fear as the sudden sound of steps pounded loudly down the tunnel that led to the way out.

The Ogre who'd been watching over them must have heard the key screeching and returned to see what was going on.

Now was my opportunity. I'd show them all what I was capable of.*

I didn't have time to think of a clever plan. I didn't even have time to think of a stupid one.

Like Aunt Prudence in the attic when she grabbed the silver horn, I simply seized the nearest thing that came to hand, which was the bottle of green liquid on the table, and waited for the running feet to draw nearer.

When the Ogre rushed into sight, I **BOPPED** him hard on the back of the head. He fell face down on the ground and lay still.

"Surely you've not killed another Ogre?" declared Stoop wearily. "What did I tell you

*Probably.

about capturing them alive? There's going to be so much paperwork after this."

"I haven't killed any Ogres! The other one got up and ran away, remember? And this one's still breathing. . . isn't he?" I added nervously as he showed no sign of getting up.

Nancy checked his pulse, and confirmed that the Ogre was not even a bit dead.

Still, there wasn't a moment to lose. This monster too could wake at any moment.

We had to get the townsfolk out of there.

Four Become
Three Again

The key had cooled down a little, so I tossed it
to Humbert, who unlocked the cage and
let out all the people who'd been caught
by Boffin.

Amazingly, they weren't terrified of him,
as we'd been on first meeting the bear.
They didn't seem to notice that he was
a bear at all.
The townfolk just thought
he was a big hairy
man with overgrown
fingernails.
One lady asked
him where
he'd

bought his fur coat. Another recommended the name of a good hairdresser. The rest simply declared that they'd quite like to go home now, if that was all the same to us, because they'd been locked up in a cage for quite a while now without bathroom facilities and were at **Bursting Point**.

Humbert was delighted. He'd always been too scared to venture into town, he said, in case everybody screamed and ran away, which is one of the six reasons why he had all his shopping, magic harps and balls of wool included, delivered direct to his door.*

"You'd better go with them," I said to Humbert, as the townsfolk all started trooping noisily towards the exit, seemingly unaware that they were still in grave danger. "They're bound to be nabbed by the Ogres again if no one's looking after them."

Humbert readily agreed.

He also promised to warn the Mayor that

---

* You'll have to ask him the other five reasons yourself. They never came up in conversation.

there was a small army of Ogres up here on the hill, and that King's Nooze would soon turn into an All You Can Eat buffet if they didn't take steps to defend it. I was sorry to see him go, but it was reassuring to know there was one person . . . well, bear . . . who appreciated the seriousness of the situation.

"Good luck, Jack!" said Humbert as he herded the last of the townsfolk out of the cave like absentminded goats, before turning one last time to wave goodbye. "I'm sure we'll be seeing each other again soon."

I hoped he was right, but the truth is that I may have saved the townsfolk* but I was no closer to finding Dad and no closer to knowing what had brought all the Ogres together in one place.

Perhaps this Ogre might finally provide me with some answers?

Together Nancy, Stoop and I knelt down and all three of us heaved and shoved at the Ogre in

* For now.

an effort to roll him on to his back.

At first it felt like we were three beetles trying to move a fallen tree.

The Ogre didn't budge an inch.

Then Nancy thought of tickling him, and that seemed to do the trick.

The Ogre wriggled so much as we tickled him under the armpits that he rolled over by himself.

I saw at once that it wasn't Boffin. This Ogre had a huge bump between his eyes.

The sort of bump that might be made by a rock. The sort of rock that might be fired from a catapult. The sort of catapult that might belong to a boy called . . .

"Jack," said Stoop with a shake of his head. "You're in for it now."

There was no denying it. This was the same Ogre I'd knocked out in the garden that morning, and I very much doubted that he was going to be pleased to see me again.

Groaning

Somehow we managed to haul the Ogre into the armchair, and I set about looking for a collar to loosen, because I'd heard once that that's what you're meant do when someone's fainted. (I'd never been on a **First Aid For Monsters** course, but I could only guess the same technique would work on them.)

It wasn't much help in this case.

The Ogre's shirt didn't fit him very well. The collar was stretched so tightly round his bulging neck that it was like trying to unfasten a very strong and determined python.

I tried fanning him with my monster hunting book instead.

The Ogre's eyes were opening sluggishly, like mussels peeping out of their shells, not sure what they were going to see.

When what they saw was me, the Ogre began to produce the most extraordinary sounds from deep inside his throat as if his tonsils were grinding together like boulders.

"Is he speaking Ogrish?" I asked Stoop.

"No," Stoop replied. "It's more like your basic moaning and groaning. But he definitely seems to be trying to say something to you. Put your ear closer to his mouth so that you can understand what he's saying."

"What if he bites me?" I said in alarm.

"Don't worry, I've got a spare hankie in my bag. I'll be able to mop up the blood so that it doesn't leave a stain on your tunic."

"That's not what I'm worried about!"

As it happened, I didn't need to risk being bitten. The Ogre was able to force out three little words from between his enormous lips.

Those words were "know", "you" and "I", though he put them in a different order. They wouldn't have made any sense otherwise.

"I know you," he said in a thick voice.

"Me?" I said nervously.

"Yeah, you. Your name's . . ." He frowned as he struggled to remember it. "Jack! That's it. Jack. You hit me this morning. With a rock."

"Did I?" I said.*

"Yeah, you did. It hurt."

He rubbed the bump between his eyes, before realising that he now had another more recent and much sorer one on the back of his head to match it. He tried to rub the new bump too, but it was too painful to touch.

The Ogre fixed me with a sorrowful stare.

"Tell the truth," he said in his gravelly voice. "You did that one too, didn't you?"

I was forced to admit that it was true.

"I should've known." He frowned. "But why are there two of you all of a sudden?"

*Even more nervously.

"There isn't," I said. "There's only me."

"You're wrong. There are definitely two. No, wait. There are three now."

He sank back into the chair, groaning some more.

"I don't feel well," he said, reaching for the bottle that had struck his head so forcefully and helping himself to a deep swig.

"Never mind that," said Stoop impatiently. "Tell us all you know. Where is this **Abominable General Meeting** of yours going to be held? When does it start? What are you all up to? I'm warning you. You'd better tell us, or you'll suffer worse than a couple of bumps on the head. I'll pull out your innards and turn them into outtards! I'll pluck out your tonsils and play table tennis with them! I'll . . . I'll . . . Jack, what do you think you're doing?"

Reinforcements

What I was doing was pulling Stoop to one side
to have a quiet word in his ear.

"Are we actually allowed to do any of those
things?" I said, because he'd insisted from the
start that we weren't supposed to mistreat
monsters and it did sound as if what he was
suggesting would hurt quite a lot.

Stoop looked sullen.

"Strictly speaking – no," he confessed. "Less
strictly speaking – still no. But the Ogre doesn't
know that, does he? If he's scared enough, he
might talk."

"Well, I don't think you should be mean to

him," I said. "I feel bad enough about knocking him out once, never mind twice. He's already seeing double. Plucking out his tonsils would be adding insult to injury."

"It'd be even worse than that," said Nancy. "It would be adding INJURY to injury.

"Or injury to injury to injury, if you count both times I knocked him out," I said.

"Or injury to injury to injury to injury, if we also count both tonsils," Nancy added.

We could have gone on like that all day.

Thank goodness we didn't.

"I'm with Jack," Nancy said. "The Ogre's our prisoner and he has rights."

"What do you suggest we do?" snapped Stoop. "Ask him nicely? Offer him a free sandwich for every snippet of information?"

I did wish Stoop would stop mentioning food. I was reminded that I hadn't eaten all day because I'd missed breakfast and Stoop hadn't offered to shared any of his food.

My stomach rumbled so loudly that it sounded like a hundred woolly mammoths snoring. I immediately apologised.

"That noise isn't coming from your belly," said Nancy. "If it was, you'd definitely need to see a doctor. Something else is going on."

Nancy and I dashed down the tunnel to investigate where the noise was coming from.

In the distance, we saw a long, snaking line of Ogres from the cave up above marching down the hill and across open ground into the nearby wood.

That was the rumbling I'd heard.

They were being joined by a multitude of others arriving from all directions, on foot, on pogo sticks, on motorbikes.

As we watched, an enormous bus pulled up, and more Ogres tumbled out, some carrying picnic baskets, as if they were planning on making a day of it. Three Ogres were floating down from the sky on parachutes.

I'd had more practice at counting than Humbert, but even I soon lost track of how many there were. Every Ogre in the country seemed to be converging on this spot.

"The AGM must be about to start," I said, as the last of the Ogres disappeared into the trees. "We have to get in there and find out what they're plotting."

"We can't stroll into a crowd of monsters unannounced," Nancy pointed out. "We'd stick out like the sorest sore thumbs ever."

"Our Ogre wouldn't," I said.

We resolved to head back inside and try to persuade the Ogre somehow to help us get into the AGM.

Two surprises awaited us. The first surprise was that Ogre was out cold again. The second surprise was that Stoop was no longer Stoop.

Look Under B

I'd only met Stoop that morning, but he'd definitely had a maximum of two ears then.

Now he had three – no, five – no, nine!

New ears were sprouting from the side of his head like mushrooms in a damp garden. The sound of them popping into life was like popcorn in a sizzling pan of oil. There was also a massive orange wart where his nose had been a short while earlier, and his beard had grown wilder and thicker than a garden belonging to someone with no lawnmower.

He'd expanded so much, in all directions at once, that he no longer looked like a monster hunter at all.

He looked like . . . **an Ogre**.

What was weirder still is that he didn't seem to have realised yet, as he demanded to know what we were staring at.

"Stoop, I need to show you something."

I took off my helmet so that he could see his reflection in the shiny metal.

He stared at himself in horror.

"Is that . . . me?"

"Well, it certainly isn't one of us," said Nancy. "What happened?"

"I haven't the foggiest idea," Stoop said. "I was just standing here, having a drink of this delicious concoction when . . ."

Stoop stopped.

He looked down at his hand.

He was holding the green bottle that I'd hit the Ogre with when he rushed into the cave.

Stoop's voice rose with excitement.

"Can it be true?" he said, holding the bottle up to the light to look at the label.

There on the front was a picture of a skull and crossbones, and the letters BB.

"Berserker Brew," he announced with relish. "I've always wanted to try some of this stuff. There were rumours once that they had a crate of it in the cellar at the Monster Hunting Arms, but it turned out to be ginger beer."

"What in the name of mischief and mayhem is Berserker Brew?" I said.

"Have a look in *Monster Hunting For Beginners*. You'll soon see!"

I opened up the book and turned to B.

"Banshees . . . Barghests . . ." I said, turning the pages quickly. "Bigfoot . . . Blue-Caps . . . Bullbeggars . . . no, I've gone too far." I flicked back to the right part. "Here it is."

Berserker Brew

A drink originally invented by Ogres and stolen by the Vikings to give them courage before going into battle. Ogres have been known to feed it to their babies to make them grow up strong and extra revolting.

Warning: Berserker Brew causes side effects in anyone who isn't at least 37 per cent monster, including unwanted flatulence,* green tongue, and/ or temporary transformation into Ogre form. There have been at least three documented cases where the transformation proved irreversible.

"That's all we need!" I said in despair.

"Yes, it is, Jack," said Nancy mysteriously. "It's exactly what we need. It might even be the answer to our problems."

What could Nancy possibly mean?

---

* That's what people who don't like to use words like "burping" and "farting" call burping and farting.

Something Bigger

"Think about it," said Nancy. "We need to get into the Ogres' secret meeting, right?"

"Right."

"And we agreed that's not possible without the help of an Ogre, right?"

"Right."

"What's the opposite of left?"

"Right again," I said.

"Precisely!" said Nancy. "So why shouldn't we BE the Ogres!"

"Brilliant plan!" Stoop exclaimed. "But aren't you worried about the side effects? Trust me, unwanted flatulence is no laughing matter when it gets out of hand."

He followed it up with the loudest – and, I'm afraid to say, smelliest – demonstration of 'unwanted flatulence' I'd ever had the misfortune of being in the same cave as.

"That's just a risk we'll have to take," I said, grabbing the Berserker Brew from his clutches before it caused another eruption of noise and fumes inside his trousers.

I thought I was going to pass out as I removed the cork and sniffed what was inside. It reminded me of the smell of Ogres' feet, and that wasn't in my top ten list of favourite smells. It wasn't in the top thousand.*

This wasn't the same as squaring up to an Ogre with a catapult. What if the Berserker Brew didn't work on me? What if it worked too well, and I couldn't turn back?

I didn't want to be an Ogre for ever, even if they were a protected species.

But a monster hunter had to do what was

* *Even the smell of wet dog came in at No. 846.*

necessary to get the mission finished.

"Here goes nothing," I said.

Rubbing the rim of the bottle on my sleeve to wipe off any spit, I lifted the bottle to my lips and nervously took a sip.

It wasn't as bad as I feared. Though since I'd expected it to taste like a cross between ear wax, itching powder, and the curried worm and earwig quiche that Aunt Prudence had once forced me to eat, that wasn't hard.

I took a second sip.

I felt the liquid trickling down my throat and into my belly. It was so hot that I felt like I could burp fire if I tried, but I didn't try. Belching flames is very bad manners.

Something was definitely happening.

I held up my hands. My fingers were fattening fast like sausages. My skin was bulgier than old bark.

I looked down and saw my body growing massive as the Berserker Brew took effect, like a balloon filling with air.

A very ugly balloon.

With glasses.

And . . . horns?

I reached up nervously.

Sure enough, I had horns.

Three of them.

"How do I look?" I said when it was done.

"Utterly revolting!" said Stoop, and he meant it as a compliment.

"My turn!" said Nancy.

"Are you sure?" I said. "There's no reason for us both to risk getting stuck permanently in Ogre bodies."

"You didn't think I'd let you take the risk alone, did you?" she said. "What kind of friend would I be if I did that?"

There was no stopping Nancy when she'd made up her mind.

She snatched the bottle of Berserker Brew from my hand without hesitation and drank.

It took longer to work on her than it had on me. She was taller, for one thing, which meant that the liquid had further to travel to reach every part of her body.

When it did –

"Look at her go!" exclaimed Stoop.

Nancy was expanding at such an alarming rate that it would soon be a squeeze to get out of the cave if she didn't stop. I had to take a few Ogre steps back to make room for her.

Her glasses barely managed to stay perched on her swelling nose.

Unlike Stoop, the number of Nancy's ears did at least remain at two, but they were both so humungous that she'd have needed to use whole sheep for ear muffs.

Nancy and I were now ready to go

Stoop reluctantly agreed to stay behind and watch over the Ogre in case he came round again and tried to warn his fellow monsters that we were on to them.

The Berserker Brew had made him bigger, but he still wasn't as Ogre-big as we were.

He begged for one last sip of Berserker Brew all the same. I tossed the bottle to Nancy to keep it out of his reach. We would need every drop to stay in our horrible new shapes.

Into the Woods

Finding the exact location of the Ogres' secret meeting didn't take much doing. Monsters can't go anywhere without leaving a mess. We simply had to follow the **Trail of Destruction**.

Nancy and I made sure to take regular gulps from the bottle so that the transformation didn't wear off too quickly – but the mixture wouldn't last all day.

How long did Ogre get-togethers last? School assemblies took forever. Even if this meeting was half as long as that, half of forever was still time enough to be rumbled.*

We kept our spirits up by taking turns at burping so that the smell of Berserker Brew in

*And eaten.

the air would mask the scent of fresh human.

I started off by burping the alphabet. Nancy then joined in by burping backwards from ninety nine to one. Afterwards, we burped the national anthem together.

The Berserker Brew made the experience even more fun by magnifying the strength of our burps, proving that not all flatulence is unwanted.

Soon, we heard the Ogres. It was the second worst sound I'd ever heard.*

I took a deep breath and prepared to walk the last hundred yards to **Almost Certain Doom**, before remembering that Ogres don't walk. They slog. They trog. They stump.

We slogged and trogged and stumped as best we could. Nancy also threw in a bit of trudging for added effect. We'd both seen enough Ogres today to know how they moved.

Blocking the path was a new Ogre. It was his job to cross names off a clipboard as the guests

---

* *The very worst sound is children in school all playing the recorder at the same time.*

arrived, which
is tricky when you
can't read or write and
have an iron railing
instead of a pencil.
Nancy handed
me the bottle, and I
took a quick mouthful
of Berserker Brew to stop my new
monstrous hands shaking.

All of a sudden, another horn poked out of
my head, but the Ogre either didn't notice or
else these things happened so often that he
didn't think it worth mentioning.

The Ogre looked me up and down.

"I don't think I've seen you before," he said.
"What's your name?"

"Nog," I grunted back, because it sounded
like the sort of name an Ogre would have.
"What's yours?"

"Dung," said the Ogre, scribbling on his

clipboard enthusiastically with the iron railing, "but that's none of your business."

"So why did you tell me?"

Dung was so confused by big words like "you" and "me" that he couldn't think how to answer that, even after bashing his head a couple of times with the iron railing.

He turned his attention to Nancy instead.

"What about you?" he demanded.

"I'm with Bog," she said.

I nudged her sharply.

"Did I say Bog?" she corrected herself. "I meant Log . . . Jog . . . no, Nog. I'm Bog."

"How do you spell it?"

"B for Beastly. O for 'Orrible. G for Gruesome. It's short for . . . er . . . Sludge. Look, there I am on the list."

She jabbed a stubby finger at the clipboard.

That seemed to be enough to satisfy Dung. He waved Nancy and me . . . or Nog and Bog, as we now were . . . through without further ado.

I couldn't believe our luck – if getting closer to a bunch of monsters who hated everything about human beings apart from the taste of them raw could be considered lucky.

It was too late to turn back now.

Ear We Go

It was only when we stepped into the clearing that Nancy and I realised what a dangerous thing we'd done by coming here alone.

The whole area was thick with Ogres.

I almost swooned at the combined smell of their stinkiest bits.

I recognised some of them because they'd been sleeping in the cave earlier. Some I only recognised from my nightmares.

Nancy and I squeezed into place at the back of the crowd, hoping not to be noticed.

At last we were going to find out why the Ogres had slogged and trogged from all over the country to meet at this spot.

It was Boffin who spoke first.

"Friends, Ogres, countrymonsters," he said, stepping up and hollering for attention, "lend me your ears!"

One Ogre sitting near the front tore off an ear and threw it at him.

"That's not what I meant," said Boffin, "but thanks all the same, I'll save it for supper."

He tucked it down the front of his shirt to keep it nice and musty.

"First of all," he began, "I want to welcome all those of you who've made it here today for this **Abominable General Meeting**. I can see plenty of deplorable old friends in the crowd. There's Clag and Skulk, Fusty and Creak, Chunder and Nark. Not forgetting Norman, whose parents hated him so much they couldn't even be bothered giving him a proper Ogre name when he was born."

The Ogres all cheered at the sound of their names, except for Norman who probably didn't like to be reminded that his name was less terrifying than a ghost train with no ghosts, because that's just an ordinary train.

"I also want to pay tribute," Boffin continued, "to absent friends who can't be with us today. Like Scab, who was too dim to find his way here and is sitting at this very moment in a tunnel in the London Underground wondering where you all are."

The Ogres clapped in appreciation at such magnificent stupidity beyond the call of duty.

"Now I'm sure you're all wondering why you've been brought here today," Boffin said when the applause died down.

"No!" cried the Ogres slow-wittedly.

"I'd like to tell you . . . and I would if I knew but I don't. But I do know someone who does. So put your hands together – all four, if you have them – and give a warm Ogre welcome to the amazing, one and only, thoroughly loathsome and nasty . . . Aunt Prudence!"

Deep Fried Knees

It couldn't be . . . but it was.

I gaped in astonishment as a familiar figure in flying goggles and black hobnail boots stepped out from the trees.

"That's her!" I whispered to Nancy. "She's the one I was telling you about."

Aunt Prudence's head swivelled in our direction, as if sensing my presence.

Our eyes met briefly.

I held my breath, afraid that she might recognise me even in my changed state, before she shook her head like a soggy dog, and turned back to the assembled gathering.

The Ogres didn't have a clue who Aunt Prudence was, but cheered loudly anyway, until she raised a hand and demanded silence so that she could start talking.*

"Friends, Ogres –!"

She got no further before the same Ogre as before tore off his other ear and tossed it to her, which was bad for him because he now couldn't hear a thing, but good for Boffin, who now had another ear for supper.

"I know I don't look like a monster," said Aunt Prudence, "but trust me, I am every bit as gruesome and unpleasant as you are." (She wasn't kidding!) "My mother was an Ogre and my father was an accountant called Simon. From him, I inherited a fondness for maths."

"Weird," muttered Nancy and I together.

"From her, a lifelong taste for deep fried knees, and a hatred of all human beings."

"Boo!" I shouted, wanting to show that I loathed people as much as the next Ogre.

* That had always been one of her favourite hobbies, along with squeezing out a dirty dishcloth on my face when I was sleeping because the thought of me having pleasant dreams enraged her.

Once again her eyes glared me into silence, and I couldn't help wondering anxiously if they lingered on me a bit longer than before, perhaps wondering why an Ogre was wearing such a uselessly small pair of glasses.

"Ever since I was a girl," Aunt Prudence went on eventually, putting aside whatever doubts she had about my true identity, "my mother would tell me bedtime stories of **Ye Good Olde Days** when Ogres ruled the land.* Ogres did what we wanted, when we wanted, to whoever we wanted, and if anyone complained then they'd soon get a close up view of our lateral and central incisors.** The Ogre King alone was said to eat a hundred children before breakfast, and that was when he WASN'T hungry. When he WAS, he'd gobble up a whole school."

Aunt Prudence had their attention now. They might not care about history, but there was nothing they admired more than an Ogre who'd

---

* She wasn't wrong about that. A man called Geoffrey of Monmouth wrote the same thing in his book, History Of The Kings Of Britain, nearly a thousand years ago.

** Those are fancy names for the teeth at the front that bite the tough bits off food.

bagged a steady supply of fresh meat.

"The Ogre King was the most powerful monster this country had ever seen," Aunt Prudence went on, eyes gleaming like jellied eels as she warmed to her theme, "and he'd be ruling it to this day if it hadn't been for the humans. They finally got fed up of being light snacks and raised an army of monster hunters to overthrow the Ogre King in battle."

The Ogres roared in fury. I could see that they'd never heard this story before.

"The battle went on for days. The Ogre King munched down hundreds of the enemy . . . he gobbled up thousands . . . he nibbled three more . . . and then disaster struck. The next monster hunter that he swallowed must have been past his Eat Before date. The Ogre King was poisoned. He fell lifeless to the ground and his Ogre army lost heart. They retreated to the wild places, where the Ogres have been ever since. The humans were victorious."

The Ogres bellowed with horror.

Some of them burst into tears.

"Do not despair, my fellow eyesores!" said Aunt Prudence. "I discovered that the Ogre King wasn't dead. He was only sleeping under the ground, waiting for the glorious day when he'd wake up and take back his rightful kingdom. Then Ogres would rule again. No more people! No more monster hunters!"

"What'll we have for dinner if there's no more people?" muttered one Ogre in the crowd, because he might not know much about ancient kings and battles but he did like eating.

"Quiet!" yelled Aunt Prudence. "I haven't spent my whole life being a **Menace to Society** every Monday to Friday, and searching for the Ogre King at weekends, just to be interrupted now when I'm getting to the good bit."

"It's about time," muttered one brave Ogre before the others shushed him.

It must have been his lucky day. Aunt Prudence didn't hear what he said.

"Look down," she commanded the Ogres. "Look down, and tell me what you see!"

What's in a Name?

One after another, the Ogres started yelling out what they could see when they looked down.

"Our feet?"

"Grass?"

"A large puddle of wee?"

A quick glance in the direction of that particular voice confirmed the worst. The Ogre who'd spoken was splashing in it merrily.

Aunt Prudence shook her head at each and every suggestion.

"I'll give you one more guess," she said.

"Beetles?"

"Buttercups?"

"Beef Wellington stew?"

"That's three guesses," said the Ogre who'd suggested beetles. "She said we only had one."

"We weren't sure if she meant one each, or one in total," the others replied. "Can we get some clarification on the rules, please?"

"Clouds?" suggested a further Ogre who'd misunderstood Aunt Prudence's instructions entirely and was staring up at the sky.

Nancy didn't need more clues.

"She's talking about the Ogre King!" she whispered to me. "Don't you see? That must be how the town got its name. It's not King's Nooze at all. It's King's SNOOZE. The Ogre King is sleeping under our feet!"

Whisper or not, Aunt Prudence heard her.

"You've got it in one!" she blared. "Come backstage after the show to receive your prize. I'd always suspected that he had to be buried round here somewhere, because of the name. Then one day I made a great discovery.

I mightn't have known EXACTLY where the Ogre King lay – but I heard about somebody who did. All I had to do was steal the secret from them. Confident that my **Dastardly Plan** would work, I invited all the Ogres whose names I could find in the phone book to come here today to share the moment when the Ogre King reclaimed his kingdom. That moment has come! Friends, Ogres, countrymonsters" – Boffin waited hopefully for a third ear, but it never came – "stand back and, without further ado, or any other kind of ado, I will wake the Ogre King!"

Rise and Shine

The Ogres did as they were told, falling back until the clearing was empty except for one wicked aunt in flying goggles and black hobnail boots. Silence fell. Even the wind didn't dare to interrupt Aunt Prudence.

I thought she was going to perform a magic spell to wake the Ogre King.

Instead, she simply reached into her jacket and took out a shiny brass alarm clock.

It wasn't any shiny brass alarm clock either.

It was MY shiny brass alarm clock.

She must have stolen it from my room in anticipation of this great moment.*

Aunt Prudence wound up the clock and set it

* No wonder I'd overslept that morning!

down on the ground.

The Ogres waited expectantly.

Then they all jumped as the alarm went off.

"That's not going to work," I whispered to Nancy, because alarm clocks might sound loud when they go off in the morning and it's cold and you really don't want to get out of bed, but surely the ringing wouldn't wake a monster as dreadful as the leader of all Ogres?

I was wrong. Aunt Prudence had done her homework. She knew that an Ogre's ears are very large, so any sound grows bigger, like a voice through a loud hailer. The alarm clock only needed to be placed at the exact right spot next to the Ogre's ear to do the trick.

The grass began to convulse.

So did I.

Presently, the whole clearing was shaking like jelly on a trampoline. Something was happening. Right before my eyes, I saw a huge hand push its way out of the ground.

A second soon followed.

The knees came next.

Dirt flew into the air as the Ogre King set his gargantuan hands on to the earth and pushed himself upright, shaking his great knobbly head and blinking in the bright light.

Then he rose to his feet.

He was more than three times bigger than the biggest Ogre I'd seen so far, and at least seven times uglier too, though I wouldn't have believed that was possible five minutes ago.

On his head, he wore a huge metal crown. Soil had gathered inside the crown during his long sleep, so that it looked now like a walled garden.

This was so much worse than I'd feared. An

army of Ogres was bad enough. But an army of Ogres led by the Ogre King himself, with Aunt Prudence at his side?

That was a horror beyond imagining.

My hand reached for Nancy's.

Nancy's reached for mine.

It was comforting at least to have someone to share the last second before the Ogre King took up where he'd left off hundreds and hundreds of years ago.

I was just sorry that we couldn't have been friends for a bit longer before the world ended.

"**Your Bigness**!" said Aunt Prudence, stepping forward and bowing her head. "Tell us what you would have us do!"

Porridge?

The Ogre King looked down at Aunt Prudence.

"Was it you who woke me up?" he said in a voice that boomed more loudly than three thunderstorms having an argument in the middle of an earthquake.

"Indeed it was, **Your Enormousness**," she said proudly.

"Well, I wish you hadn't," he said, his voice softening as he opened his mouth wide and yawned. "I was having a lovely dream about eating apple pie. It was all sprinkled with sugar and covered with thick clotted cream. I do love a dollop of clotted cream. I don't suppose you have any on you?"

Aunt Prudence looked almost as confused by the mention of clotted cream as Dung had been by big words. This clearly wasn't what she'd expected when the Ogre King woke up.

"I'm afraid I don't, **Your Outsizeness**, but I do have a whole cageful of people in a variety of flavours nearby if you're peckish? On my instructions, Boffin has been collecting them for a few days now, so that you can enjoy a slap up meal when you wake."*

"People?" said the Ogre King with a shudder. "You want me to eat people? I don't eat people. That's what Trolls do. I'm not a Troll, am I? Don't get me wrong, I'm not one to judge on appearances, but Trolls are rather on the ugly side, not handsome like me."

"With respect, **Your Colossalness**, I've made an extensive study of this subject, and it does say in all the best and oldest stories that the Ogre King regularly ate more people at a single sitting than most Ogres eat in a week."

* I decided this wasn't the best moment to tell her I'd already rescued them.

"You can't believe everything you read in stories. Those ones were all made up. Mainly by me," said the Ogre King. "I just wanted to frighten the humans into leaving me alone. I certainly wouldn't want to eat people just after waking up. I prefer porridge."

"PORRIDGE?" cried Aunt Prudence in shock.

"What's wrong with porridge?"

"It's disgusting, that's what's wrong with it," said Aunt Prudence, and for once I was on her side. Porridge is much too slimy.

The Ogre King's brow furrowed.

"You haven't all been eating people while I've been asleep, have you?" he asked.

Aunt Prudence couldn't help looking slightly embarrassed.

"Just a few," she admitted. "Maybe more at Christmas and special occasions."

"That is naughty of you," the Ogre King said, and he sounded like one of those teachers who insist they're not angry, just disappointed, when you get into trouble.

The Ogres were beginning to mutter among themselves. The Ogre King was meant to lead them into battle and take back his ancient kingdom, not hold out his hand for the birds to perch on, which is what he was now doing.

"Enough!" cried Aunt Prudence, sensing their discontent. "The Ogre King is simply drowsy after his long sleep. He's forgotten what it is to be a good Ogre, and by that I mean a very bad Ogre. Pick up your clubs and cleavers, and anything else that makes a good **THWACK**, and follow me, your new leader! First we will make mincemeat of the townsfolk down below. Actual mincemeat, the kind you put in pies. Then it's on to the rest of the country for Round Two. Soon England will be ours again! Can I count on your support?"

"No!" the bewildered Ogres answered, but it didn't matter that they didn't understand.

They knew when there was wickedness afoot.

They stamped their feet and prepared to set off for battle.

What were we going to do now?

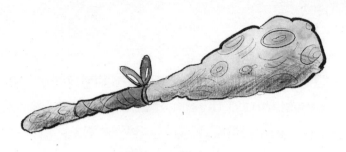

Groof!

Nancy and I did our best to join in as the Ogres tore down trees to make clubs, but our hearts weren't in it, and the bottle of Berserker Brew was dry. We'd swigged down the last drops as Aunt Prudence roused the Ogres to action. Looking at Nancy, I saw that the concoction was beginning to wear off

Her ears were much bigger than they'd been before she'd changed, but she'd only have needed a couple of lambs as ear muffs now, not fully grown sheep.

My own body that had resembled a balloon a short while ago still looked like a balloon, but a balloon that was deflating.

"We have to get out of here," said Nancy.

"Don't worry," I said. "I have an idea."*

I raised my hand and coughed.

"Excuse me," I said, "may I please use the bathroom?"

A shocked silence fell on the gathering.

Even the Ogre King looked outraged.

No self-respecting Ogre would ask to go to the bathroom. If they needed to go, they simply went, wherever they were.

In bed. In the middle of important meetings. The Ogre who'd been splashing earlier in a puddle of his own wee had demonstrated that. They'd even have gone while sitting in the bath, if they ever had baths.

Aunt Prudence fixed me with a stare of pure malice.

"**FEE FI FO FUM**, I smell the blood of a pesky one," she exclaimed, seeing through what was left of my disguise. "It's Jack, together with some girl I've never met but who I'll bet is every

---

* I don't want to spoil what happens next, but let's just say that if someone tells you they "have an idea", you shouldn't get your hopes up.

191

bit as irritating as he is. I should have known it was you all along. Who ever heard of an Ogre wearing glasses? Who ever heard of TWO Ogres wearing glasses? Don't let them get away!"

There was nowhere to run. If there had been, we would have run there.

Nancy and I got to our feet and prepared to make our **Final Stand** as the Ogres lunged towards us, finally realising that we weren't Ogres at all, but were actually made of food.

If we'd been normal size, we might have been able to dodge out of their grasp, but there was still a trickle of Berserker Brew in our veins and it wasn't fading fast enough. We weren't used to being so clunking and clumsy.

We managed three steps before falling down with a pile of Ogres on top of us.

I tried to shout: "Get off!"

All that came out was: "Groof!"

I then tried to say "groof" again, but more Ogres had landed on the heap, knocking the breath out of me, and I couldn't say that either.

"Stop," I heard the Ogre King pleading. "You'll hurt the little chaps."

"I'm not a chap," came Nancy's muffled voice from somewhere inside the tangled pile of Ogres. "I'm a girl."

"Sorry. I didn't mean any offence."

"None taken," she said. "I just thought I should mention it for the sake of accuracy."

No one was listening to the Ogre King anyway. Another voice had risen above the din.

"Never fear, Stoop is here!"

Peeking out through a tangle of legs, I saw the monster hunter, back to his normal size, leap into the fray, whirling his sword around his head, not caring a fig at that moment about not being allowed to hurt monsters.

His only thought was to save us.

He wasn't by himself either.

Wading into battle at his side was the Ogre with two lumps on his head, one at the front, one at the back. He was wielding a club and using it to bash the head of any Ogre who stood in his way until those other heads all bore bumps every bit as big as his own.

Of all the Unexpected Turn Of Events, this was the most Unexpected and Turniest.

Why was the Ogre suddenly on our side?

Had he come to finish off what he started that morning with Aunt Prudence?

Most of all, why was he so much smaller than I remembered, and getting smaller still with every moment that passed?

There was no doubt about that part. The Ogre was shrinking so fast that the other Ogres were now towering over him.

He could no longer reach their heads, and had to content himself with bashing their knees instead, which, to his credit, he set about doing with **Undimmed Enthusiasm**.

The smaller he got, the less like an Ogre he

looked. His yellow tusks were shrinking like ice cubes in the sun. His face was losing its mouldiness, revealing less daunting – and more familiar – features.

"DAD!" I exclaimed, because that's exactly who it was. It would have been a strange thing to shout if it wasn't.

We Get Knotted

Questions were swarming and buzzing around in my head like bees on motorbikes.

Why was Dad an Ogre? He'd never made a habit of turning into a monster before.

I was bound to have noticed.

Where had he been all this time?

Most of all, would I ever get the chance to find out what was going on before the Ogres did what Ogres do best,* and brought my adventure to an unpleasant and chewy end?

Stoop and Ogre-Dad – or maybe that should be Dad-Ogre, I wasn't sure which was the correct way to describe him – were sparing no effort to pummel their way through the throng

* Or should that be worst?

to reach us, but there was only so much that they could do against that many opponents.

They were quickly overpowered.

"Shall we eat them now?"

"I want a leg!"

"You always get a leg!"

"I want a wing."

"They haven't got any wings."

"Who ate all the wings?"

"I just want some clotted cream," said the Ogre King mournfully.

"Will you stop blithering on about clotted cream, Your **Dim-Witted Immenseness**?" shouted Aunt Prudence. "I'm in charge here and I say no one's eating anyone till King's Nooze is flattened. These four'll do for pudding after we've eaten all the others, and there's not the itsiest, bitsiest, teeniest, tiniest thing you can do to stop me, Jack!"

She ended her speech by dancing a frantic jig, then tweaking my nose for good measure, because she really was a very odd woman.

"You'll never get away with it!" I shouted as Ogre fingers pinched my collar and hoisted me in the air, though I can't think why I bothered saying that, because there was every chance that she would get away with it.

I felt myself being wound tightly in a length of rope, as if I was a cut finger and the rope was a sticking plaster, before being dropped roughly on the ground.

I sat there, **WRIGGLING** furiously to get free, but it only made the rope tighter.*

The next moment Nancy was plonked down next to me, followed by Stoop, and lastly Dad, all knotted up the same way.

It was some comfort to see that everyone I cared about was human-sized and human-shaped again,** but the relief didn't last long.

Together, we could only watch helplessly as the Ogres charged down the hill towards King's Nooze, with Aunt Prudence at the head of the

---

* *I'll say one thing for Ogres. They do know how to tie a good knot.*

** *For humans, that's definitely the best size and shape to be.*

army, blowing tunelessly on the silver horn that she'd stolen from my house, with the Ogre King tagging along reluctantly at the rear.

Only Boffin was left behind to watch over us, and he seemed almost as upset about it as we were, even if it was for different reasons.*

I crossed my fingers that the townsfolk had listened to Humbert and taken all Necessary Precautions to defend King's Nooze, or they'd be well and truly done for.

* It's not every day that you get the chance to munch down on an entire town.

Me Versus Dad

"We are in a pickle and no mistake, Jack," said
Dad with a shake of his head as the last blasts
of the horn died away. "Didn't I always tell you
that the world was a **Perilous Place**? I bet
you wish you'd listened to me now, and stayed
at home where it's safe, instead of dashing off
into danger without a second thought."

I couldn't believe my ears.

I'd been so happy to see Dad again. I'd been
looking forward to telling him all the things
I'd done since becoming a monster hunter. I
wanted him to be proud of how I'd managed
on my own since he vanished.

I wanted him to say: "Good job, Jack – and

yes of course you can have a pet snail, though they really do have lots of teeth,* so I wasn't wrong when I said they might bite you."

Instead he was STILL treating me as if I couldn't be trusted to leave the house without Round The Clock Supervision.

"Who says I WANT to be safe?" I cried.

Now it was Dad's turn to mistrust his ears.

"You mean you like not knowing if you'll make it all the way to dinner time without being the main course?" he said in amazement.

"I'm not saying it isn't scary," I said, "but it's exciting as well. You can't ask me to give it up now. Our old life was so boring, Dad. We never had any fun."**

I waited for him to protest again, but Dad simply looked sad.

I knew that expression. I'd seen it on his face lots of times. It was the one he always wore when he was thinking about Mum, and I felt bad for being the one to make him feel that way

* *Between 10,000 and 12,000 on average, if you must know.*

** *It wasn't true, but you say things that you don't really mean when you're upset.*

after he'd waded into a whole gang of Ogres without hesitation to save me.

But he had to understand. I wasn't the same Jack that I'd been last week when he waved me off to school for the last time.

It was right there on the first page of *Monster Hunting For Beginners*.

It's your job to save the day when monsters start misbehaving.

I didn't know if saving the day was too tall an order in our present tied-up situation. All I knew is that, if **Life As We Knew It** was about to come to an end, I didn't want it to end without finding out what this strange day had all been about. And for that, I needed all the facts.

It was time to hear Dad's side of the story.

Dad's Side

It was a long story, and it was made even longer because Nancy and I kept interrupting Dad to comment or ask questions.*

I could have written it down exactly as it happened, with all our comments and questions kept in. But if I did that we'd be here all day. Instead I'm just going to summarise the Main Points so that we can then get back to that whole "monsters about to attack King's Nooze" thing.

Basically, it went like this.

As I suspected, Aunt Prudence wasn't really my aunt. Dad hadn't known she existed until a few weeks ago when she called him up

* Stoop didn't need to. He'd heard the whole thing on the way to the wood to rescue us.

offering to buy the map of the Ogre King's last resting place, which was hidden in our attic.

Dad had no idea how she'd found out about the map, but he explained to her politely (because he had good manners) that it wasn't for sale at any price.

She'd immediately vowed revenge and slammed down the phone (because she had no manners at all).

That was the last he'd heard from her until she pulled up alongside him in a van one day and demanded directions to the nearest butcher's shop. Dad was kindly pointing her to Bloody Joe's in the High Street when she leaped out, threw a sack over his head and bundled him into the back of her van, before driving for hours to a tumbledown house in the Middle of Nowhere,* and locking him inside.

There he stayed for days on end with nothing to eat but a mint humbug that he found in

---

* Or it may have been slightly north of the Middle of Nowhere. He wasn't sure. Everywhere looks the same in Nowhere.

his pocket, and nothing to drink but bottles of Berserker Brew, because the house was full of them. That must have been where Aunt Prudence kept her personal supply.

("Lucky beggar," muttered Stoop.)

Naturally, not being 37 per cent Ogre, Dad promptly changed shape. But what else could he do? He had to drink something, or he'd have shrivelled up like an octopus who's booked a holiday to the Sahara desert by mistake.

Luckily, the more Berserker Brew that Dad drank, the stronger and more Ogre-like he became, until eventually he was able to break down the walls of that tumbledown house and make his way back home. Imagine his shock when he realised that the woman who'd kidnapped him was now living there!

What was worse was that she'd found the map and was about to set off for King's Nooze to wake up the Ogre King.

Dad's blood ran cold. Mum had made him

promise before she died never to let the map fall into the wrong hands, and it couldn't have fallen into wronger hands if he'd put an ad in the newspaper inviting the owner of the **World's Wrongest Hands** to come and help themselves to it. He'd immediately grabbed her and demanded that she give it back. He wasn't really going to eat her, he said, though he did admit that she looked very tasty.*

That's when I hit him between the eyes with a rock and he fell on top of our house.

("Nice shot, by the way," he added.)

When he came round, Dad was afraid that I'd fire another rock at him before he got the chance to explain who he really was, so he hid behind the house next door and eavesdropped on Stoop and I as we found the map in the rubble, before following us to King's Nooze, where I promptly knocked him out a second time.

Only when the effects of that blow began to wear off did he remember again who he was.

---

* Most people do when you've only had one mint humbug to eat all week.

He told Stoop, and they promptly ran into the woods to try and rescue Nancy and me.

I think that covers the whole story, but if there's anything you're still not sure about, feel free to drop me a line and I'll try to tie up any loose ends. Nothing is more annoying in a book than unexplained plot holes.*

This jigsaw only needed one final piece before it was complete.

"What on earth was a map of the Ogre King's last known whereabouts doing in our attic in the first place?" I exclaimed.**

Dad looked sheepish.

That meant he was embarrassed, not that he looked like an actual sheep – though that would definitely still be an improvement on looking like an Ogre.

"I'm sorry, Jack," he said. "I haven't been straight with you. I've been keeping a secret all these years. You see, the thing is . . . Nell and I were monster hunters too."

* Apart from long, detailed descriptions in stories of what people and places look like. Who cares so long as there are pictures?

** You've probably thought of that question already.

Pulling My Leg

I couldn't have been more flabbergasted if I'd found a shark swimming in the toilet, or an actual bird's nest in a bowl of bird's nest soup. It was like finding out that a dead slug is the world record holder at the 100-metre hurdles.

Dad COULDN'T be a monster hunter!

As I've mentioned before, he wasn't the kind of person to get caught up in adventures

If he ever wrote a book of all the exciting things he'd done in his life, I'd always thought it would have fewer chapters than *The Ogre Book Of Good Manners*.

His idea of Living Dangerously was to try out a new brand of tea bags.

Now it seemed that was just one more thing I'd been wrong about.

"You're pulling my leg," I said.

"I'm really not," said Dad. "I couldn't with my hands tied."

"Me neither," said Stoop indignantly. "I'm nowhere near your leg!"

"I don't think that's what Jack means," Nancy tried to explain, but it was no use; Dad was talking again, and I simply never got the chance to clear up the confusion about my leg.

"The truth is, Jack, that you come from a long line of monster hunters. That's why we called you Jack in the first place. Jack the Giant Killer was a distant ancestor on your mother's side of the family. It was she who first got me into this business. She actually tricked me into becoming her apprentice by giving me a copy of *Monster Hunting For Beginners*. You should've seen the gleam of triumph in her eye when she realised that I'd fallen for it.* I'd never have taken the

* *I knew that look all too well.*

210

job otherwise. When we met, I was training to be a palaeontologist. That's someone who studies fossils."

"I know!"

What did he think I did all day at school? Stare out of the window, daydreaming?*

"I don't blame you for not believing me," said Dad as he saw me struggling to take in all this new information, "but I can prove it."

Squirming inside his ropes, he managed to squeeze one hand into his pocket, and took out a small pile of photographs.

"Look, here's a picture of her fighting a Kraken. (That's me on the left, hiding underwater.)

* I only did that half the time.

This is her trying to hypnotise a three-headed bogeyman with an eyeball tied to a string of mouldy spaghetti. (Trust me, you don't want to know all the horrible details. I still have nightmares about it sometimes.) And here she is, having a wrestling match with . . . well, I'm not quite sure what that is."

"Some sort of shapeless blob with too many mouths," I finished for

him as Dad trailed off.

Dad sighed wistfully.

"Just between me and you, Jack, I wasn't much good at monster hunting. I was better at running away. It was your mum who did most of the fighting. She did love a good scrap."

"Nell was the best," agreed Stoop. "You know, Bob, they still have her picture up on the wall at the headquarters of the International League of Monster Hunters. I had no idea you were their son when I took you on as my apprentice, Jack."

"Jack's the reason we gave it all up," Dad said. "When we settled down to start a family, I begged Nell that the only way any child of ours would be safe was if there were no monsters around. I hoped in time that Jack would take after me and choose a safer hobby. Like stamp collecting. Or bullfighting. Nell knew better. She always said he'd follow in our footsteps. That's why she told you so many stories about monsters, Jack. She wanted you to be ready when the time came. I just wish she was here now. She'd know what to do. She always did."

I should have been angry with him for keeping the truth from me for so long when it all confirmed what I'd always known deep down about having a **Taste for Adventure**.*

But I was tired of fighting with him.

He couldn't help the way he was either. He'd only been trying to protect me.

"Don't worry, Dad," I said, feeling at that moment as if I was the grown-up and it was he who needed comforting, like me when I was small and woke from a bad dream. "I'll think of a plan to get us out of here. I'm not Mum's son for nothing."

"You know what, Jack?" said Dad. "I really do believe you will. I'm just glad you got Nell's brains instead of mine, or we'd be toast. Burnt

* As well as that aforementioned taste for sausage rolls.

toast. The worst toast."

What I didn't admit was that I'd been racking those brains ever since we were tied up, and I still hadn't come up with a foolproof plan to save the day.* What was the point of finding out I came from a long line of monster hunters if that line was now to come to an end?

* I hadn't even come up with a plan that was whatever the opposite of foolproof is.

The Benefits of Not Existing

If we were going to get free, we needed Boffin to untie us, but that was easier said than done.*

The Ogre had been sitting sulkily under a tree with his arms folded ever since the others rampaged down the hill. How was I meant to persuade a moody monster to set us free when eating us was all he had to look forward to?

I tried to remember all the things I'd learned about Ogres that day.

They were big.

They were dumb.

They had extremely smelly feet.

Of those three facts, only the second one offered any chance of being much use.

I decided that the direct approach was best,

* Everything is, when you think about it. Saying you'll do something is always easier than doing it.

and called Boffin over.

"I need your help to get out of these ropes," I said, giving him the widest smile I could without splitting my cheeks. "They're hurting my wrists."

I held out the knots for him to loosen.

The Ogre looked almost disappointed in me for thinking that my plan might work.

"How stupid do you think I am?" he said.

"Pretty stupid I was hoping."

"Well, I'm not," said Boffin. "Aunt Prudence left me in charge and I'm going to make sure that you're still here, ready to be gobbled up, when she gets back."

"You can't keep us here against our will!" declared Nancy hotly. "Don't you know it's against the law to tie up children?"

For the first time, the Ogre looked scared.

"Are you really . . . children?" he asked, his eyes widening in fright.

"Of course we are," Nancy said. "What

did you think we were – a pair of Giant Fartdoodles?"

"But you can't be children," Boffin said. "Children don't exist."

"We don't?" I said, startled, because I was fairly certain that we did.

"I'm glad you admit it," said Boffin, not realising that my previous remark had been a question rather than a statement. "It's a well-known fact. Children are just things that mummy and daddy Ogres invented to make little Ogres behave. My parents were always telling me to stop bashing my brother Baffin with a lamppost when we were babies, or a child would come and get me in the night."

Boffin shuddered at the memory.

I suddenly felt more hopeful again. I had an idea. And this one might just work.

"But if Nancy and I don't exist," I asked, "why have you tied us up? Tying up things that don't exist is a waste of good rope."

"I hadn't thought of that."

"In fact," I went on, "if we really don't exist then you might as well untie us right now."

"I don't suppose it can do any harm if you really don't exist," said Boffin, loosening the bonds around our wrists. "I'm not untying him, though," he added, glowering at Stoop. "He's a monster hunter. I know they exist."

"Of course you mustn't untie him," I said as Nancy and I used our free hands to unfasten the ropes around our feet and stand up. "That would be a very foolish thing to do. But it doesn't matter if I do it, does it, because I don't exist?"

"Good point," said Boffin as I set to work.

"Come to think of it, if I don't exist, it doesn't even matter if I use these ropes to tie you up instead, does it?"

"I don't like being tied up," Boffin said.

"But I don't exist, remember?"

"Oh yeah, I forgot for a moment."

"Lend me a finger," I said, winding the rope round and round the Ogre's legs and pulling it tight. "I need to tie a knot."

Boffin helpfully stretched out a finger so that I could make a neat bow.

Then I started to wrap the rest of the rope round his chest, pinning his arms tight.

"I'm glad you don't exist," said the Ogre, "or I'd be feeling really silly right now."

"Ogres are even more dimwitted than I thought," said Nancy as she bent down to free Dad from his bindings too.

The Ogre, finally realising that he'd made a mistake, struggled to get loose.

"It's not fair!" he protested. "I'll make an official complaint to the **Council of Monsters**. It's totally against regulations to be captured by non-existent beings. I liked it better in the old days when you just used to kill us."

"So did I," said Stoop, "but what can we do about it? I'm only a lowly monster hunter, and

you're a clodding great people-eating chump
with a brain no bigger than a grain of sand.
We'll both just have to get used to it."

Boffin sobbed with shame as we
dashed down the hill towards
the rising din of battle.

Wreck and Ruin

By the time we reached King's Nooze,
the battle was in full flow.

Charging into the town square alongside
Nancy, with Dad and Stoop a little way
behind, both puffing and holding their
sides, I saw that the Ogres had already
caused **Considerable Destruction** to
the surrounding buildings.*

Most of the windows were smashed, and
the crooked clock tower had never been
more crooked. The butcher, the baker and
the candlestick maker would have made a
fortune if they'd started selling debris and

---

* *That's one of the worst kinds of destruction you can wreak. It's far
more serious than Minor Destruction, if a lot less damaging and
expensive to fix than Total Destruction.*

wreckage, because that's all that was left of
their shops.

The flea market was also in ruins, and most
of the fleas had fled, which made sense when I
thought about it, because, if anyone should be
good at fleeing, it's fleas.

My eyes searched for Humbert, desperate for
confirmation that the bear hadn't come
a cropper since I'd seen him last.

I needn't have worried.

"There!" said Nancy, pointing upwards.

Looking up, I saw that Humbert had led
the townsfolk up to the roof of the Town Hall,
because that was the biggest and strongest
building for miles around, and they were

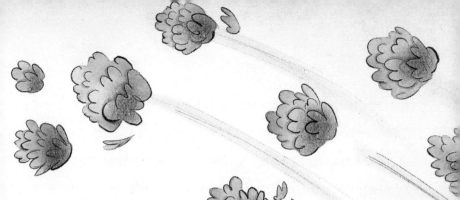

now busy
pelting cabbages
at the Ogres
who'd congregated below,
waving clubs and cleavers, as Aunt
Prudence ordered each fresh attack.

Yesterday had been market day
so there was no shortage of suitable
ammunition, and the townsfolk had no
qualms about hurting the Ogres because
they didn't know that the International
League of Monster Hunters had rules about it,
and wouldn't have cared at that moment even
if they did. Survival came first.

"What a waste of good grub," said Stoop,
eyes gaping in horror at all the cabbages flying

through the air like spherical wingless birds.*
"I'll never live it down if the Boiled Cabbage
Appreciation Society gets to hear about this. I
was elected Life President last month."

I tried telling him that the cabbages were
being sacrificed in a Good Cause, but it wasn't
in Stoop's nature to look on the bright side.

The Ogres were in an even fouler mood,
because they hadn't managed to scoff a single
local yet, and were regretting not gobbling us
up when they had the chance.

Every so often, one of them would try to
sneak up to the door, only to be forced back by
a volley of vegetables, because Ogres aren't very
skilled at moving stealthily.*

They retreated to the other side of the square
to regroup.

The only one who wasn't involved in the
fighting was the Ogre King. He was sitting
down with his back to the Town Hall, chatting
pleasantly to the people on top about how all

* So nothing at all like birds really

** You wouldn't be either if you were the size of an elephant
that's just eaten a bus.

this had once been fields, and apologising for the other Ogres' bad behaviour.

"Wait there!" Humbert cried happily when he caught sight of us. "I'll be right down."

The Ogre King raised his huge hand for the bear to hop on, before lowering him gently to the ground, where he hurried over to join us.

I politely introduced the bear to Dad, and they all shook hands and paws, and remarked how nice it was to meet, and wasn't the weather lovely for this time of year, until Stoop stamped his foot and said weren't we forgetting something?

"Is it somebody's birthday?" said Humbert.

"I'm referring to the battle," Stoop snapped. "How are we going to defeat all these Ogres?"

"I knew there was something I had to tell you, Jack!" the bear said to me. "I've remembered where the magic harp is."

Beginner's Pluck

"You have?" I said hopefully, because, if anything would help right now, a Magic Anything was categorically it.

"The harp wasn't in the cave at all. I actually sent it to be mended a few days before the Ogres burst in," Humbert said. "The strings kept breaking when I tried to play it. Harps can be fiddly when you have paws."

"Where is this shop?" interjected Nancy.

"Right over there," Humbert said, pointing to The Old Shop of Curious Things.

I feared the worst, but the shop seemed to have escaped unscathed, either by pure chance, or because Ogres have more respect for curious old things than you might think.*

"We have to get in," I said.

"No problem," said Nancy. "Follow me."

To my surprise, she walked straight up to the entrance and took out a key from her pocket. This key didn't cry out, like the one hanging on the wall in the Ogres' dungeon.

It said nothing whatsoever as Nancy slid it into the keyhole and turned it with a soft click.

"This is Mum's shop," she said, opening the door and stepping inside, ushering us to follow quietly. "She bought it when we came to live in King's Nooze. I help her to run it when I'm not at school. What do you think?"

The Old Shop of Curious Things lay before us in all its agreeable jumble and clutter.

There were statues and spoons and antique bicycle wheels and tennis rackets and wooden hat stands and iron boot racks and brass coal scuttles and wobbly tables set with silver goblets and earthenware pots and shelves lined

* I suspect it was the former reason.

with urns and pitchers and paintings on every wall except for the walls that had mirrors on and boxes filled with coins and racks of vintage clothing and cabinets stuffed with gemstones and trinkets and rings.

"When did you say that you sent it back to be mended?" Nancy asked Humbert.

"Last Tuesday," recalled the bear.

"Then it should be in here."

Nancy led the way to a store room at the rear of the shop. There, sitting in the corner, tied with string, waiting to be unwrapped, was a large brown paper parcel shaped like a harp.

It had to be Humbert's.

If it wasn't, it was a Staggering Coincidence, and Staggering Coincidences are hard to wrap neatly.

Nancy picked up the parcel and handed it to me. Now I had what was needed to put the Ogres to sleep and save King's Nooze.

Without waiting for doubt to set in, I stepped

out of the shop into the town square, coughing loudly to get the Ogres' attention.

If anybody had told me that morning that I'd be deliberately trying to get a small army of monsters to turn their ravenous eyes in my direction, I'd have said that they were cracked. What I'd longed for was adventure and excitement, not a close encounter with mouthfuls of teeth.

Monsters are as easy to distract as dogs and instantly stopped waving their clubs and swivelled to fix their Ogre eyes on me.

"You are absolutely sure this will work, right?" said Nancy uneasily, as Stoop drew his favourite axe just in case.

"Nope," I said, "but it's our **Only Chance**."

I set down the harp-shaped parcel on the cobblestones and tore off the brown paper.

The harp only had three strings left, and two of those were looking wonky. But three is still better than two, and it's definitely better than one, unless you're counting bruises, in which case none is the best number of all.

I began to play.

That is to say, I would have done, if I'd known how to play the harp. Unfortunately, I'd never had any lessons.

The moment I put my fingers to the strings, the first one snapped with a loud twang.

"It's curtains," said Stoop gloomily, as the Ogres smiled at us with greedy expressions.

Surely I hadn't come this far to fall at the last hurdle?

Changing Tune

"Why don't you look in your book?" came a jeering voice from the top of the Town Hall. "You know the one. It's for BEGINNERS."

I looked up and saw the Mayor jiggling so hard with laughter that his top hat nearly fell off. It was almost as if he wanted me to fail.

I waited for the other townsfolk to join in the laughter . . . but they didn't.

"Leave him alone," they said, turning on the Mayor. "He's doing his best. That's more than you've ever done."

I felt touched at their faith in me, but what could I do if the harp didn't work?

Then it came to me.

The Mayor was right about the answer being in *Monster Hunting For Beginners,* but I didn't need to look inside it. I already knew what the book said about dealing with Ogres with the aid of a magic harp.

See Jack and the Beanstalk for details.

Once again, I ran through the story of that other Jack who sold a cow in return for some special beans that grew overnight into a huge beanstalk that rose to the sky, and how he climbed up it to a Giant's castle in the clouds, and stole a hen that laid golden eggs and . . .

"A magic harp that plays by itself!" I clicked my fingers. "That's it. I don't have to learn to play the harp. The harp already knows what to do. I simply have to ask it nicely."

I picked up the harp.

"Please, magic harp, will you play for me?"

"I thought you'd never ask," the harp said.

The two remaining strings began to quiver, and sweet music filled the air like pollen on a summer's day, except that music doesn't make you sneeze.*

"I think it's working," whispered Nancy as contented grins appeared on the Ogres' faces.

What worried me was that the smiles didn't say "I'm feeling so sleepy that I could lie down immediately and have forty winks" so much as "Oh look, here's dinner."

"Why aren't you falling asleep?" I said.

"Haven't you guessed yet?" said Aunt Prudence smugly. "Magic harps only put Giants to sleep, not Ogres."

"Oops," said the harp.

"Get them!" ordered Aunt Prudence.

* Unless you're allergic to it, in which case it might.

Ogres or Not?

There was nothing for it but to fight.

Dad managed to grab the iron railing that Dung had mistaken for a pencil, and used it as a makeshift sword to charge into danger, still determined to protect me at all costs.

Stoop, weapons in both hands, hammered at the Ogres merrily, all rules about not hurting Ogres forgotten in the joy of the fight.

Nancy picked

up the fallen cabbages and hurled them with Unerring Accuracy at the enemy. Her best shot hit Aunt Prudence square on the nose to a chorus of loud cheers – some of them from the Ogres, who were starting to get tired of being bossed around by a leader who wasn't even a full monster, just half of one.

Even Humbert, who wasn't cut out for fighting, was faithfully unravelling balls of wool and crisscrossing the square with lines of thread in a valiant effort to trip up the Ogres as they bungled and blundered about, having as many punch-ups with each other as with us.

Everyone was playing their part, but our luck couldn't last. There were too many Ogres to fight. One by one, my friends had been backed into a corner, out of ammunition and unable to escape. I had to think fast another time.

At the back of my mind, hiding like a mouse in a tub of cream crackers, was something that Stoop had mentioned earlier when he was explaining the difference between Ogres and Giants and Trolls.

He'd said that Ogres could change size and shape when they felt like it.

Changing shape – could that be the answer?

"Why are you doing this?" I yelled up at the rampaging monsters. "You're Ogres! This isn't what Ogres are meant to do."

That made them stop.

"It isn't?"

"Of course it isn't. Don't you remember what the Ogre King said when he woke up? He said that Ogres don't eat people. Trolls do . . . Wait a minute! I've just thought. If you want to eat us, then that means you must be Trolls, right?"

The Ogres scratched their heads in confusion. Some of them were so confused they even scratched each other's heads.

"Are you sure?"

"Of course I am," I went on. "He also said that Trolls are really, really ugly, and look at yourselves. You're **REVOLTING!**"

"That's true," the Ogres said proudly. "We are. It's one of our best features."

"But if we're Trolls," one of them finally figured out, "doesn't that mean we should turn to stone in sunlight?"

"So it does." I pretended to be astonished. "How clever of you to work that out for yourselves."

"Don't listen to him!" shrieked Aunt Prudence. "It's a trick!"

It was too late. Being able to change shape was the Ogres' undoing. Just believing that they were Trolls was enough to start the process of transformation.

One by one, they turned to stone.

Some of them tried to hide from the light, but the sun was better at hide and seek than they were. It played the same game every day with the clouds and every night with the moon.

In a few seconds, the street was crowded with

huge lumps of rock where a moment ago there had been an army of Ogres.

Only Aunt Prudence was left, because she was just half an Ogre and that's not Ogre enough to be duped so easily.

"It's just you and me now, Jack," she said.

With a roar of hate, she made her move, determined to finish me off **Once And For All**.

The Back-Up Plan

"Stop, everyone," I said as the others stepped forward with their weapons drawn. "It has to be me."

Deep down, I'd always known that it would come to this. The adventure had started with me and Aunt Prudence.

It had to end with us too.

"Be careful, Jack," said Humbert as they reluctantly fell back. "She's tricky, that one."

Didn't I know it!

I strode forward alone to meet her, wondering why she was smiling.

"You're probably wondering why I'm smiling," she said as we came face to face.

"No."*

"Fibber," Aunt Prudence said. "I'm going to tell you anyway."

I thought she might.

"I'm smiling because the map showing the last resting place of the Ogre King wasn't the only thing I found in your attic last night. I discovered lots more interesting scraps of information among your mother's papers. Did you know, for example, that the first Mayor of King's Nooze was actually a Knick-Knack?"

This wasn't the moment to get into a discussion about Knick-Knacks, but, for the sake of scholarship, here's the entry for those who are interested:

I might usually be honest, but I felt that a fib was forgivable. I didn't want her to think that she could read my mind. She already had the Upper Hand, being bigger and more at ease with extreme violence.

Knick-Knacks

Knick-Knacks are the most miserable of all monsters. Their main weapon is making people feel bad about themselves. Never ask a Knick-Knack what it thinks of your new haircut. They'll always say they hate it, even if they don't. When they borrow books, they always make sure to blot out every second word on the last page in order to ruin it for anyone else who wants to read it. This is particularly infuriating if it's a murder mystery, because the only reason to read one of those is to find out whodunnit.

"It was thanks to your mother that I discovered the last piece of information I needed to ensure my **Fiendish Plan** succeeded. You're probably also wondering what that is."

There was no point pretending I wasn't.

I wouldn't have been able to carry it off.

"I found out," said Aunt Prudence, "that there wasn't only an Ogre King in **Ye Good Olde Days**. There was an Ogre Queen too."*

The Ogre King drew in his breath sharply.

"I was really, really hoping that she'd been forgotten," he said.

"Was she bad?" I said.

"Badder than a pint of milk that's been left out in the sun too long and started to curdle."

"That IS bad."

"She gave us Ogres a terribly wicked name. It was my own fault, in a way. When I started putting out all those stories about eating people, she decided to try one to see what they tasted like. Soon she couldn't get enough of them. I'd never have married her if I'd known what she was like, but I was young and in love. I thought she'd change."

"So that's it," I said to Aunt Prudence. "You're going to bring back the Ogre Queen

* *Geoffrey of Monmouth mustn't have known about her. Either that, or he was saving her up for the sequel,* History Of The Queens Of Britain, *but never got round to writing it.*

from her long sleep as well."

Aunt Prudence shook her head.

"Not even an alarm clock could wake up the Ogre Queen after what happened to her," she said with relish. "One day the Ogres got fed up with her and baked her in a pie."

"It's what she would have wanted," the Ogre King said wistfully. "I didn't have a slice of it myself. Having your own wife for dinner would have been wrong, however wicked she was . . . but the others said she was delicious."

"Speaking for myself, I'm glad they ate her," said Aunt Prudence. "I wouldn't want any competition to be Top Ogre. That's right, Jack. I'm going to take the Ogre Queen's place. I had rather hoped that the Ogre King and I could rule the land together once he woke up, but he proved to be a bumper disappointment. You know what they say. If you want something done properly, do it yourself."

What did she have up her sleeve now?

Queen Prudence

When you say someone has something up their sleeve, it normally just means that they're up to no good. In Aunt Prudence's case she really did have something up her sleeve. She reached inside it and pulled out a small golden crown.

It glinted in the sun as she held it aloft.

"This is what gave the Ogre Queen her fiendish power," she gloated. "It was lost for centuries, but I learned from your mum's notes that the crown was hidden in a nook of that old oak tree stump in the centre of King's Nooze the whole time. All I had to do was reach in and take it out. There were some mice in there, using it as an exercise wheel, but they soon scarpered when I threatened to chop off their tails and use them as bootlaces."

Before anyone could stop her, Aunt Prudence lifted the crown and set it on her head. At once, like my tin helmet had done, it began to grow. As it grew, so did she.

Nancy and I had shot up when we took the Berserker Brew. Even Stoop had got a bit bigger. But Aunt Prudence didn't stop growing when she reached Ogre size. She went on growing, and the crown expanded with her.

She grew bigger than the clock tower.

She grew bigger than the Ogre King.

She was so big that her hobnail boots filled the town square. Everything went dark as she blotted out the light. I could hardly see her face, she was so far above me.

Unfortunately, that situation quickly changed as she reached down and grabbed hold of me in her fist, lifting me high in the air the same way that Dad-Ogre* had picked her up that morning

* Or Ogre-Dad. I'm still not sure which one it is.

247

in the garden.

The others rushed forward and tried to make her put me down, but they were like a gang of sardines attacking a killer whale.

I couldn't believe that she was going to win at last.

I fought as best I could, but she was too strong. I knew what she was going to do.

Aunt Prudence opened her mouth wide and prepared to drop me inside.

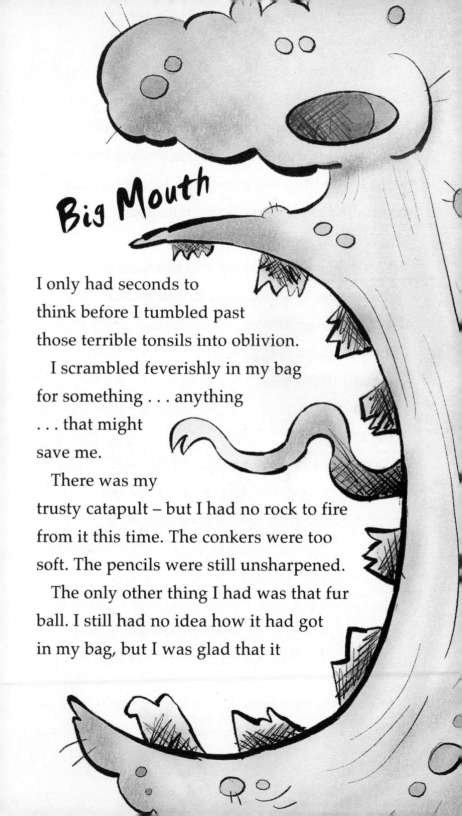

Big Mouth

I only had seconds to
think before I tumbled past
those terrible tonsils into oblivion.

I scrambled feverishly in my bag
for something . . . anything
. . . that might
save me.

There was my
trusty catapult – but I had no rock to fire
from it this time. The conkers were too
soft. The pencils were still unsharpened.

The only other thing I had was that fur
ball. I still had no idea how it had got
in my bag, but I was glad that it

had. It was only small, but so was I. Sometimes small is enough.

I dropped it into Aunt Prudence's mouth.

She must have been drinking Berserker Brew, because the moment it touched her wet tongue the fur ball puffed up like a foam sponge on contact with water.

It took her another moment to realise that she had something unpleasant in her mouth. The effect was immediate.

She coughed.

She spluttered.

She cuttered.

She sploughed.*

"Why does it taste so sickening?" she screamed through all her spluttering and coughing and sploughing and cuttering.

"Most things do when they've come out of a cat's stomach," I said.

Had Aunt Prudence been able to say more, I imagine that she would have said something like "**EUUURRRGHHH**!" That had been

---

* No one likes hairy food, as Stoop had pointed out earlier.

my first reaction when I found the fur ball in my bag. In her case, it would probably have had far more Es and Us and Rs and Gs and Hs.

As it was, she couldn't speak at all.

Huge racks and rents took hold of her unnaturally swollen body as she tried to spit out the giant fur ball, but it only went in deeper. Her hands flew to her throat in panic.

That was good, because it meant she let me go. No, wait, that wasn't good, because it meant she let me go.

I began to fall.

The ground was a long way down, but it was getting much closer much faster than I would have liked. I couldn't be sure of landing on a soft bear this time.

I shut my eyes tight.

It would be bad enough being splattered without having to watch it happen.

At the very last moment, just before I hit the cobblestones, I found that I was . . .

FLYING!

Winging It

I should probably point out that I hadn't suddenly sprouted wings and learned to fly. That would've been too improbable for words.

I was flying because I'd landed on the back of something else that could fly – and what was even more amazing is that the something I'd landed on was a dragon.

It was only a small one, but even the smallest dragon is a welcome sight when you've been told that they don't exist at all.

It's even more welcome when said dragon is saving you from a nasty splatting.*

This dragon had bright red scales that

---

* Those are my least favourite kinds of splatting.

sparkled in the sun like hot rubies as I was borne up into the air again in a whoosh of wings and a wild wind in my hair.*

We flew twice round the crooked clock tower, watching in delight as Aunt Prudence bent double and proceeded to hack up the disgusting fur ball like a cat.

It shot from her throat and stuck to the side of the Town Hall before **SLIIIIIDIIIING** down the wall disgustingly.

In a frenzy, she started looking about for a certain boy called Jack so that she could stuff the fur ball down HIS throat in revenge.**

The dragon sped off, before her swirling arms could swipe me from my seat, while my friends down below followed on foot.

Moments later, we glided gently to earth on the edge of town, and I tumbled off the creature's back, unsteady on my feet for a moment, like when you get off a roundabout and your head won't stop spinning.

* As if it wasn't messy enough to begin with.
** That's me, in case you haven't been paying attention.

The dragon bowed low before me.

"Cadwallader at your service," he said solemnly in a Welsh accent.*

I suddenly felt shy now that I was nose to snout with a real dragon.

"I hope I wasn't too heavy," I said.

"I'm like you, Jack. I'm tougher than I look," said Cadwallader. "I once carried a tractor to the Isle of Man and back for a bet."

"What did you win?"

"A year's supply of firelighters. Sometimes a dragon needs a little help getting his fiery breath going on cold mornings."

The sound of running footsteps** brought Nancy and Stoop and Dad and Humbert racing to our side.

They all pulled to a halt and stared in wonder as they neared Cadwallader.

"Well, I'll be danged," said Stoop. "Dragons do exist."

"You really didn't know?" I said.

* Probably because he was Welsh.
** And paw-steps.

"How would I? They're not on any of the official monster hunting lists."

"I'm as sure as any dragon can be that I'm the last one," said Cadwallader. "Since the day I popped up as a baby out of a pile of ash and saw that I was alone, I've scoured the world for others of my kind. Without success, sadly. Most people who see me just imagine that they're dreaming."

"What a stroke of luck you were flying by at the right moment to catch Jack," said Nancy.

"It wasn't chance," the dragon said. "I came because Jack called."

"Did I?"

"Well, someone did," Cadwallader said. "Didn't you blow the horn?"

"I don't have one," I said . . . but I definitely knew someone who did. "Was it long and made of silver, by any chance?"

"That's the one."

I hadn't blown it, but Aunt Prudence had. It

was the horn she'd found in our attic at home. The one she'd thrown at my head, and later sounded before heading into battle.

I smiled at the knowledge that it was Aunt Prudence's own actions which had saved me.

"I gave it to your mother from my own personal treasure trove. Nell saved my life once, but I begged her never to reveal that dragons are real. I promised to return the favour if she or any of her family was ever in danger. All they had to do was blow the horn, and, wherever I was, I'd come to their aid. How else do you think I knew your name, Jack? I'd recognise Nell's son anywhere."

It felt right that Cadwallader had come. Everyone who mattered was here together.

Surely, I thought as I reached for my copy of *Monster Hunting For Beginners*, there had to be some way in those wondrous pages that could help us defeat a new Ogre Queen?

In alarm, I saw that the bag was empty.

Same Difference

"The book must've slipped out of my bag as I fell through the air," I exclaimed. "I'll have to go back and get it before it too falls into the wrong hands. Namely, Aunt Prudence's."

"No need," said Nancy.

She stepped forward and presented me with a familiar-looking black book.

"I saw it drop," she said. "Better still, I know that everything falls in a straight line unless something stops it. That's called gravity. I simply had to look on the ground at Aunt Prudence's feet to find it. Which I did."

"Nancy, you're a genius!" I said.

"I wouldn't go that far, but thanks," she

laughed. Then she stopped as the smile on my face turned into a puzzled frown.

Nancy had been both right AND wrong.

The book in my hands was indeed called *Monster Hunting For Beginners*, because I was now holding it, and that was how the magic worked. But it wasn't mine.

This one was older, and the leather was more worn. There were also countless scraps of paper poking out from between the pages where they'd been stuffed for safe keeping.

I pulled out a few of them at random.

Could the Ogre King really be sleeping in the wood, as legends say? Need to return to King's Nooze ASAP to investigate further.

Ogre Queen not as bad as she sounds, or much, much worse? Ask the Oak Folk!

Must remind Bob to get more sausage rolls when he goes shopping tomorrow morning. Jack gets through so many!

Dragons? What dragons? I don't see any dragons.

I recognised the handwriting at once.

It had been on all the birthday cards I'd ever received until the person who'd written these messages couldn't send them any more.

"I don't understand," said Nancy. "Whose book is this? Is it Stoop's?"

"No," I said quietly. "It's Mum's."

Now I knew where Aunt Prudence had learned all her new information about King's Nooze. She'd found Mum's monster hunting book in the attic. Perhaps the map had even been inside its pages.

The book must have dropped from HER

pocket as she coughed up the fur ball, as mine had dropped from my bag.

Any doubt that this really was Mum's monster hunting manual puffed out like the flame on a wet match when I saw the picture which was pasted on to the inside cover.

It was a copy of my own favourite photograph. I suddenly realised why King's Nooze felt so familiar. I had been here before. I just hadn't remembered because I was so small. There we all sat on the tree stump in the town square, with the cobblestones at our feet, and the spire of the crooked clock tower peeping over Dad's right shoulder.

I knew what I had to do.

Heart racing, I opened the book.

Voice from the Past

"What's wrong?" said Nancy as my head immediately spun round in search of the voice that I was sure had just whispered my name.

"Didn't you hear that?" I said.

"Hear what?"

The voice came again.

"Jack."

I couldn't speak except to say one word.

"Mum?"

"Who else could it be, silly?" she said with a familiar laugh.

It was so long since I'd last heard it, but I'd never forgotten her voice.

How could I?

The voice was now inside my head, but it was coming from the book.

I couldn't tell if I was imagining it, or if it was real, but I suddenly understood that Mum's spirit was still there in her book, and that she'd come back to help me when I needed her most.

"Tell me what I need to do," I said.

In reply, a breeze slowly riffled the pages of Mum's book, stopping at a picture of an oak tree. This must be the tree that had stood for so long in the middle of King's Nooze, before being chopped down, leaving only a stump.

The Ogre Queen's crown had been placed inside its trunk for protection, but that wasn't the only object that had been left in there.

Squinting at the picture, I saw that there was also . . . what was that?

"It's a magnet," said Nancy.

I didn't understand. The golden crown was the source of Aunt Prudence's new power, but what use was a magnet against gold?

Gold was not magnetic.*

Mum's voice laughed again in my head.

"Things aren't always what they seem."

If I'd learned one thing today, that was certainly it. I had to trust my instincts.

I grabbed Nancy's hand and raced back to King's Nooze, certain that we had all we needed to defeat Aunt Prudence.

* See? I did pay attention in school. Sometimes.

Look in the Nook

Back in the town square, Aunt Prudence was now threatening to squish the people on top of the Town Hall between her giant forefinger and thumb if they didn't tell her where I'd gone, while the Ogre King begged her to be reasonable and sit down and talk things over.

"Jack, Nancy, do your thing!" yelled Dad and Stoop. "We'll keep this bad example to aunts everywhere busy while you get away!"

The clash of weapons and stamp of feet was all the evidence we needed that battle had begun as Aunt Prudence strove to scrunch the attackers like bugs under her outsized hobnail boots. Cadwallader, true to his word that he was at our service, whizzed here and there distracting her with jets of fire.

Nancy and I ran to the old tree stump, knelt down and peered inside the nook.

Twelve eyes glinted back at us, but they didn't belong to mice, whatever Aunt Prudence might have thought.

The eleven eyes belonged to six plump, friendly figures in bright clothing and cheeks that were rosier still.* That was my first encounter with the Oak Folk.

The oak is one of the most magical trees in the world, but don't tell them that because oak trees are already big-headed enough as it is, as anyone who's ever spent some time in their company will tell you. The only people who go on about how great oak trees are more than oak trees themselves are the Oak Folk. For generations, these tiny creatures have

* There should have been twelve eyes, but one of the people was wearing an eye patch because she thought it made her look more jaunty.

lived inside oaks as their protectors and servants. Even if an oak tree is chopped down, the Oak Folk will continue to live inside the roots. Oak Folk are friendly and kind to those who seek help, and don't really deserve to be included in a guide to monsters. Their only fault is they do go on a bit about how great oak trees are, which can get boring after the first five or six hours.

"Sorry to disturb you," I said politely, "but you don't by any chance have a magnet in there, do you?"

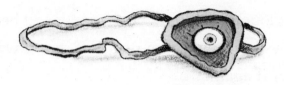

Pulling Power

"Indeed we do, Jack," said the woman who seemed to be the Oak Folk's leader, stepping forward and raising a hand in greeting.

"How do you know my name?"

"I just guessed. Most monster hunters are called Jack, in our experience."

"Except for the ones with other names," whispered a small figure hiding behind her legs, who now made his first appearance, thereby adding to the total of eyes.

"Except for those ones," she admitted, "but I wasn't talking about them."

"What do you want with our magnet?" said another of the Oak Folk, narrowing his eyes suspiciously, as if he'd been caught out before by boys borrowing magnets and didn't want to fall for it again.

"I think it will help me defeat the rotten-tempered woman who stole your crown."

That was good enough for the Oak Folk.

They disappeared into the shadows at the back of the nook and returned with the magnet, carrying it between them all because it was too big for one of them. Or even two.

"Before we present it to you for use in your noble quest to vanquish that nasty woman who

thought we were mice," the woman said, "can you please spare a moment while we tell you how great oak trees are?"

"Nothing would give me more pleasure," I said,* "but I do have my hands full at the moment, what with my aunt trying to kill me and take over the country. Maybe later?"

"We'll start making some notes."

The magnet was more powerful than I expected. As we walked back into the middle of the fight with Aunt Prudence, I had to hold on with both hands to control it as the magnet instantly detected the weapons hanging from Stoop's belt and tugged him halfway across the square, followed by a blizzard of iron candlesticks from the ruined baker's shop.

"Whose side are you on?" Stoop bellowed as he ducked out of the way of the flying rain of candlesticks.

There was no time to explain. I simply pointed the magnet at Aunt Prudence's head.

* *Lied.*

Fight and Flight

If the Ogre Queen's crown really was made of gold, all this fighting would have been for nothing. If it wasn't, we still had a chance.

The magnet pulsed in my hands as it probed for something on which to fasten.

Suddenly, I felt it latch on, as if I was fishing and something big had taken the bait.

"Where do you think you're going?" cried Aunt Prudence in alarm, hands clasping on to her crown which was now vibrating madly.

The magnet was stronger. It pulled the crown right out of her grip. It came hurtling towards me at a furious rate.

I braced myself for the impact, because the crown had grown to a considerable size while it was on her head and, if there's one thing I wasn't, it was a considerable size to match.

I could only hope that the crown had shrunk enough by the time it stuck to the magnet to avoid knocking me off my feet.

Any . . . moment . . . now.

CLANK!

The crown was back to its ordinary size. Better than that, it was in our possession.

Without the magic of the Ogre Queen's crown, Aunt Prudence was dwindling. She was already smaller than the clock tower. Then she was smaller than the Ogre King, then smaller than Humbert, then smaller than Stoop.

Smaller than Stoop?

That couldn't be right!

Her body seemed to realise that it had gone too far in the other direction and bounced back to the way it had been all along.

To guarantee she'd stay that way, Cadwallader took a deep breath and, without any need for firelighters, blew flames at the crown until the gold paint that had been covering it peeled off, revealing a cheap metal crown beneath. It began to melt until there was only a steaming grey puddle of molten liquid.

Aunt Prudence knew that the game was up.

She looked around at all the people waiting to lay hold of her . . . and fled.

She was surprisingly athletic for a woman in hobnail boots.

"Stop her!" yelled the Oak Folk.

That was just what I intended to do.

I hopped again on Cadwallader's back.*

Nancy hopped on too because she didn't want to miss the chase, and we took to the air.**

"You'll need this," said Humbert, tossing us his last ball of wool.

We swept through the winding streets of King's Nooze in pursuit of Aunt Prudence.

She glanced over her shoulder at the sound of Cadwallader's beating wings and tried to run faster, but she was no match for him.

She dodged down alleyways.

We swooped round to cut her off.

She tried hiding in the crooked clock tower.

I took out my catapult and fired a rock at the bell to make it clang. She ran out with her hands over her ears to escape the loud clamour.

There was nowhere left but the open road.

* I asked him if it was OK first. I'm not someone who just snatches lifts off dragons without permission.

** Yes, she asked permission too. The dragon said it was fine as both together us were still far lighter than a tractor, and I should hope we were!

She ran as fast as she could away from King's Nooze, but she'd never be as fast as a dragon, not even a small one.

Cadwallader flew in circles as I spooled the wool round her, until she was so snagged and ravelled that she fell face forward with a wallop.

"I think you'll find that's Jack's," said Nancy, bending down to snatch the silver horn from Aunt Prudence's pocket and handing it to me.

"I should have eaten the both of you when I had the chance!"snarled Aunt Prudence, realising at last that she was beaten.

"Thank goodness you didn't," I said. "Think of all the fun we'd have missed if you had!"

"Fun?" she said, waggling her tongue as if the very word tasted bad. "I'd rather have some good old-fashioned misery any day."

I almost felt sorry for her. But only almost. It's hard to feel THAT much sympathy for someone who only sees you as a tasty side dish.

Together Again

Back in King's Nooze, with Aunt Prudence safely in tow, we found the townsfolk inspecting the new boulders that had once been Ogres, tut tutting about how inconvenient it was going to be, weaving round them on their bicycles in future.

They were only reassured when Stoop explained to them that the Ogres wouldn't be stones for ever. The changes would wear off in a week or two when they remembered that they weren't really Trolls because they didn't live under bridges. Then they'd be taken away for rehabilitation and released back into the wild after learning how not to make a nuisance of themselves.

"Well done, Jack," said Dad, rushing forward and hugging me tightly as if I was the last multipack of his favourite crisps in the shop and he didn't want to let me go.

It was the best hug I'd had in a long time,* but I couldn't help squirming to get free. What would Nancy think if she saw me?

I needn't have worried.

Glancing over, I saw that she was fastened in someone's arms too.

Nancy's mum might have trusted her to look after herself, but that didn't mean she hadn't been sick with fright when she returned to King's Nooze in the midst of the battle and couldn't find her daughter anywhere.

"Mum would have been so proud of you," Dad said, his voice cracking. "I just wish she could have been here to see it. "

I stopped squirming, not caring any more

---

* It was also the only hug, but that's another matter.

what anybody else thought. I understood at last that Mum wasn't really gone. She'd always be here with us.

"You mean you don't really mind me becoming a monster hunter and not knowing if I'll make it to dinner time without being the main course?" I said when he finally let go, and I was pretending that I had something in my eye and had to rub hard to get it out.

"I'll never stop being scared when you're out of my sight, Jack, I can't help it, that's just the way I am. But what kind of dad would I be if I stopped my own son following his True Calling? Nell was right all along. You were born to be a monster hunter. I can see it now."

"I knew you would, in the end," I said.

"You will have to keep going to school, though," he added. "It's against the law for children to get full-time jobs."

"It's a deal," I said.

Good things come in threes.

That's what people said.

I counted the good things that had happened to me.

One: I'd made new friends who were as funny and kind as I could ever have hoped.

Two: I'd not only been reunited with my missing dad, but also found Mum, who I'd feared was lost forever.

Three: There'd be more adventures to come.

All in all, I had to admit that things had worked out pretty well in the end.

"Things usually do," Mum said.

One More Villain

That night the townsfolk held a feast under
the stars. Music was provided by the magic
harp, and cakes by the candlestick maker, who
didn't skimp on a single grain of icing sugar
in recognition of the event. Stoop was given
as much boiled cabbage as he could eat, and
no one spoiled his appetite by pointing out
that it was the same cabbage that they'd used
earlier as ammunition against the Ogres, while
Humbert was made to feel more welcome than
an unexpected present when it's not even your
birthday and Christmas isn't for months.

Everyone had finally realised that he was a
bear, and they all wanted to be his best friend,

because there'd never been a bear in King's Nooze before, and they couldn't have asked for a more likeable one to get the ball rolling.

There was even a place at the table for Boffin. The Ogre King had given him a stern talking to about Why Eating People Is Wrong, as well as introducing him to the delights of clotted cream, and the repentant Ogre had crossed his heart and promised not to devour any of the other guests if he could possibly help it.

The only one who missed the start of the party was me. I'd been sitting in a corner by myself, trying to finish off my first entry in *Monster Hunting For Beginners*.

Every monster hunter in the world would have the chance to read it once it was done.

I wanted to get it right.

I knew Mum would have helped me find the right words if I'd called on her again. That's why I'd given her book back to Dad for safekeeping. I hadn't heard her voice since, and still wasn't sure if it had been real.

It didn't matter. She had been there when I needed her most. But I had to make my own way in the monster hunting world now, and that meant having my own book back again.

I'd gone out looking for it as soon as Aunt Prudence had been taken away in handcuffs, and soon found it in the ruins of the flea market. It was a little bit dusty, but it was mine. I knew that I'd always feel incomplete without it.

A new and terrible creature had now taken its place in the book alongside all the Boggarts andBogeys, Galleytrots and Clabbernappers, Slabberkins and Old Shocks, Giant Fartdoodles and Crusted Hairy Snot Nibblers.

Aunt Prudence

Aunts are not generally evil. They can be annoying and embarrassing, and have a bad habit of buying you presents that are meant for much younger children, because they don't really notice that you're getting older. But on the whole they don't try to eat you or take over the world. Aunt Prudence is different, probably because she's half Ogre. Some might say that being half an Ogre is only half as dangerous as being a full Ogre, but in fact it's worse. Ogres are too stupid to do much damage. Aunt Prudence not only has Delusions of Grandeur, she's also clever, which makes for a deadly combination. She can be easily identified on account of her hobnail boots and flying goggles and a tendency to yell at small children simply for breathing in her presence. It's unlikely that she will pose a threat, as she has been sent to Monster Gaol for a long time for multiple breaches of the peace, but it's better to be safe than sorry.

I showed it to Dad as I took my seat next to him at the feast, reaching at last for a sausage roll and taking care not to get crumbs between the pages. He said it was my best work yet, and asked if he could rip out the page and pin it on the wall of our kitchen, where he hung all the other stories and drawings that I brought home from school.*

I didn't want to spoil the moment by reminding him that we didn't have a kitchen, because, between us, we'd managed to demolish it, along with the rest of the house.

I also wasn't sure if tearing out pages from the book was allowed.**

"I don't know what we'd have done without you, Jack," the Mayor declared, dragging me to my feet and putting his arm around my shoulder as he posed for pictures for tomorrow's **Monster Hunting News**. "I'm just glad I called in expert help before things got out of hand. Please, peasants, no need to thank me. It's a Mayor's job to put the welfare of others before himself. Vote for me!"

* Parents always exaggerate about how talented their children are. They can't help it.

**Stoop later confirmed, grumpily, that it wasn't. Any damage to official copies of the manual had to be mended at each monster hunter's personal expense.

"Put a sock in it," said Boffin. "You were the one who said we could eat them. You told us you had the fattest, juiciest townsfolk in the whole of Cornwall. He promised one of you would keep an Ogre satisfied for a week. I don't know why we believed him. I've never seen a gristlier lot in my whole life."

Half the townsfolk began to shout indignantly at the Ogre for insulting them as a supply of nutritious food. "How dare you? We're very tasty!" they insisted. The other half were staring hard at the Mayor.

"Everyone, calm down. It's stuff and nonsense, I tell you," he said, backing away. "Who are you going to believe – me, your hardworking Mayor, or an Ogre?"

"The Ogre," they replied as one.

The Mayor could see that denial was useless. His secret was out.

"Don't let them hurt me," he pleaded, grabbing hold of my sleeve. "It's not my fault. Boffin was only supposed to eat a few people. I even gave him a list of the most annoying ones that no one would miss. How was I to know every last Ogre in the country was about to descend on the town and help themselves?"

"If it's any consolation, we were going to eat you as well," said Boffin.

If the Mayor felt relief at such a narrow escape, he didn't let it show. He had other things on his mind. Like running away before the townsfolk nabbed him and presented him to the Ogre as a tempting titbit. He was last seen disappearing over the hill in the general direction of Anywhere But King's Nooze.

The townsfolk in turn begged Humbert to become the new Mayor, and he accepted, so everyone was happy. The gold chain looked very fetching next to his fur.

Last Things Last

"King's Nooze isn't such a bad place, is it?"
said Nancy when calm had been restored and
the Oak Folk were taking the opportunity to
enquire if anybody wanted to hear their **Ten
Favourite Facts About Oak Trees**.*

"I could get used to it," I admitted.

"Good," she said. "It's decided then."

"What is?"

"That you should come and live here. Your
old house has been reduced to a pile of rubble.
You don't have any friends at that silly school
of yours. Think how glad you'd be if you never
had to see Stanley Jenkins again. I've never met
that kid and even I don't like him! There's not

* *Nobody did.*

a single reason you shouldn't move here right away. Mum and I did."

Nancy's suggestion made a lot of sense, I had to admit. King's Nooze had been Mum's home when she was growing up, and it was where I'd come into my own as a monster hunter. I felt accepted here at last.

"What do you say, Dad?"

Dad pretended to think about it, but I could tell from the smile on his face that he'd already made up his mind.

"Why not?" he said.

"All this moving house had better not interfere with our monster hunting," piped up Stoop, tucking into his umpteenth bowl of boiled cabbage and only belatedly wondering why it tasted grittier than usual. "You're still my apprentice, in case you've forgotten. We have a legally binding agreement."

"We?" I said. "I thought you wanted to retire from monster hunting?"

"I'm prepared to keep working for a little while longer," Stoop said. "Just until you're fully trained, you know?"

I think he secretly didn't want to miss all this fun. He just didn't want to admit it.

I assured him that I was ready for the next adventure. Stoop said that was just as well, because it was about to begin.

He jabbed his fork in the direction of the crooked clock tower.

There stood a penguin with a letter tucked between the two halves of its beak.

This must be one of the famous carrier penguins that he'd mentioned earlier.

"Looks like the International League of Monster Hunters has another mission for us," said Nancy, because there was no way that she was going to be left behind.

"Can I come along too?" said Cadwallader, landing neatly on the back of my chair.

"How could I say no?"

I looked down at the book sitting beside me on the table. It was no longer called *Monster Hunting For Beginners*.

I wasn't a beginner any more.

The title on the front said . . .

. . . but that will have to wait for another time. Even monster hunters need a good night's sleep when they have a long journey ahead in the morning.

THE END

A message from Monster Hunting HQ

This book is for beginner monster hunters only. That's why it's called *Monster Hunting For Beginners*. If it was for little nosey parkers who should mind their own business, it would be called *Monster Hunting For Little Nosey Parkers Who Should Mind Their Own Business*. If that includes you, then don't worry. Maybe you found this book on a train, or under a bush, or it was sent to you by mistake. It happens.

(Any copies received accidentally should be returned at once by carrier penguin to the Monster Hunters Official HQ at Llanfairpwllgwyngyllgogerychwyrndrobwllllantysiliogogogoch.)

It could be that it's too late, and you've already read it. In that case, you may be wondering:

Is monster hunting for me?

We have devised the following quiz to track down new recruits. Can you tell your Stinkers from your Stonkers? Could you outsmart (or outfart) a Giant Fartdoodle? Do you have what it takes to be the next Monster Hunter? Turn the page and FIND OUT . . .

THE QUIZ!

Seven questions (one for each of the leagues that
you can travel with a single step when wearing
seven league boots):

QUESTION ONE
You come down for breakfast one day to find a strange
woman who claims to be your aunt about to be
eaten by an Ogre. What do you do?

A. Did somebody mention breakfast? That reminds me –
I haven't eaten for at least half an hour! Sorry, what was the
question again?
B. That sounds very alarming, but there's no need for
fighting, is there? Can't we all just sit down and do a nice
puzzle?
C. You'd better rescue me . . . er, I mean her . . . before it's
too late, or you'll be in BIG trouble. Being eaten would ruin
all my evil plans.
D. I'd grab my trusty catapult and run to the rescue. That's
a monster hunter's job, whether they like the person who's
about to be eaten or not.

QUESTION TWO
It's got nine eyes, three and a half noses, a bright
green tongue as long as a garden hose, and its head is on
back to front. What is it?

A. That's probably just me after drinking too much
Berserker Brew. Don't worry, I'll be back to normal again
after I've slept it off.
B. I don't even want to know what it is. Just please make it
go away before it curls up and goes to sleep in my knitting
bag.
C. No idea, but I DEFINITELY want it to join my army of
mischief-making monsters . . .
D. Wait a moment while I check out *Monster Hunting For*

Beginners to identify what it is and how to deal with it. That's what the book is for, after all . . . ah yes, here it is. It's a Nine-Eyed, Three-And-A-Half-Nosed, Green-Garden-Hose-Tongued Backwards-Headed Beast. I should have guessed.

QUESTION THREE
What are the main differences between a Giant Fartdoodle and all other species of Fartdoodle?

A. What am I – a walking encyclopedia? Go find out for yourself and stop bothering me with silly questions when I'm trying to eat.
B. Giant Fartdoodles paint excellent watercolours.
C. Fartdoodles are all pointless. They don't even have mouths, so they can't bite anyone. What's the use of a monster with no teeth?
D. Giant Fartdoodles have no mouths and eat with their bums, whereas Little Fartdoodles have no bums and poop out of their mouths so you should never ask one for directions or you'll need a bath afterwards.

QUESTION FOUR
It's lunchtime, but the only thing to eat is a huge pot of stew, and you're not sure what – or who – might be in it. What do you do?

A. Tuck in. You never know where your next meal's coming from. A monster hunter has to eat.
B. I'd rather have some honey, if it's all the same. It took weeks to get the smell of stew (and goodness knows what else) out of my nice cave after the Ogres moved in.
C. It couldn't be as nice as deep fried knees – but, as long as it doesn't taste like a fur ball coughed up by a cat, who cares?
D. Best not risk it. You don't want to end up accidentally eating people when you're supposed to be saving them. Just remember to bring a packed lunch next time.

QUESTION FIVE
Who is your all-time favourite Jack?

A. Jack the Giant Killer. He was lucky to live in a time when you could just do away with fearsome monsters without everybody getting flustered about it.
B. My good friend Jack, the newest and best monster hunter of them all, who defeated all the Ogres trying to take over King's Nooze.
C. There are no good Jacks. Not a single one. Come to think of it, I hate all boys, whatever their stupid names happen to be. I'm not that fond of girls either. I only like monsters.
D. I'm going to say Jack the Giant Killer too, but only because he was the one who started this monster hunting business and where would I be now if he hadn't?

QUESTION SIX
You're lying in bed. Looking down, you see two strange foot-shaped lumps at the bottom of the bed. What do you do?

A. Hit them with a hammer. It's best not to take any chances where monsters are concerned.
B. Ask them very nicely if they wouldn't mind sleeping somewhere else, because it's very hard to relax when there might be monsters in your bed.
C. No monster would dare mess with me when I'm trying to get to sleep after a hard day's work making other people's lives a misery.
D. They're probably just your own feet, but lift up the covers and have a look anyway, because you never can tell with monsters.

QUESTION SEVEN
What would you do if confronted by a Knocker at midnight on Midsummer's Eve?

A. Knock its block off. Yes, I know we're not allowed to kill monsters, but you can always say afterwards that you didn't really mean to do it.

B. I don't know, but my knees are already knocking just thinking about it.

C. Ask it to join you in your Fiendish Plan to take over the world. (Don't knock it till you've tried it.)

D. Nothing. Knockers are only dangerous in daylight. Everybody knows that.

How did you do?

MOSTLY As

You're definitely a monster hunter, but you are also 200 years old, so it may be time to retire and find yourself a new apprentice to take over, so that you can spend your time doing the things you love best. Like eating. And grumbling.

MOSTLY Bs

You mean well, but you're just not cut out for fighting monsters. You much prefer a nice quiet life in your cave, knitting and learning to play the magic harp.

MOSTLY Cs

Be honest. You're Aunt Prudence, aren't you? This is no place for you. A monster hunter's duty is to save people from hungry and bloodthirsty creatures, not recruit them into your plan to take over the world.

MOSTLY Ds

You are a natural monster hunter. You definitely know your Stinkers from your Stonkers, and you don't hesitate to do the right thing when people need help, even if they are sometimes very ungrateful for it.

Congratulations on completing the quiz.
As your reward/punishment, we are pleased to announce
that you will be joining Jack, Nancy and Stoop on another
epic, DANGEROUS, monster hunting adventure!
ARE YOU READY?*

MONSTER HUNTING FOR BEGINNERS 2

COMING SOON!

(Full details to be delivered by carrier penguin)

*Unfortunately by finishing this book you have already agreed to go
on the next adventure and face certain death. Sorry about that.
(But we did tell you to read the small print.)*